P9-DKD-652

The sled veered unexpectedly. Brody landed in a heap, and Lila landed with a fierce thump on top of him.

He looked up into the laughter of her eyes, the joy on her face, and he let himself have it. He let himself have this moment.

Something inside of him let go: his need to protect himself, his need to be in control, his need to not ever be hurt again.

He looked into Lila's shining face and he could clearly see she had risen to the challenge of allowing her heart to be made braver. She was *welcoming* whatever was happening between them.

He let go of his own desire to run from it. If she could be so brave, then he could be, too. It was not the kind of bravery that reached into a burning car and pulled out a woman stuck behind the steering wheel.

No, it was not that kind of bravery. That kind of bravery had its place.

But it did not hold a candle to the kind of bravery that was being asked of him now. To put his heart at risk. To say *yes* to the mystery of something bigger than he could control. To say *yes* to what was in the laughter of her eyes, and the way she had rested against his chest last night.

To say *yes* to life.

Dear Reader,

There is something about turning fifty (two days after Christmas for me) that makes a person ask, have I used my life wisely? Have I done enough? Been enough? Have I achieved the things I hoped to achieve?

Sometimes answers come in unexpected ways. As I was working on this Christmas story, I heard Josh Groban sing "The Little Drummer Boy."

It was such a beautiful reminder that we are all given a gift—perhaps humble, perhaps grand—and it is not the gift itself that matters, but how we use it.

I recall a waiter so wonderful I still remember him with more delight than the musical concert that followed; I have a hair stylist who loves her work so absolutely it is pure pleasure to see what she'll do this time; I was at a hotel in Mexico where the maid radiated good cheer and amazed us over and over by sculpting the bathroom towels into swans and boats and other creations.

If you bring your heart to what you do, no matter what that is, it becomes a gift to others. And to Him. That is my intention with each story I write. May it bring joy.

With holiday wishes,

Cara Colter

CARA COLTER
His Mistletoe Bride

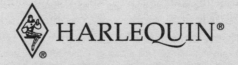

HARLEQUIN®

TORONTO • NEW YORK • LONDON
AMSTERDAM • PARIS • SYDNEY • HAMBURG
STOCKHOLM • ATHENS • TOKYO • MILAN • MADRID
PRAGUE • WARSAW • BUDAPEST • AUCKLAND

If you purchased this book without a cover you should be aware
that this book is stolen property. It was reported as "unsold and
destroyed" to the publisher, and neither the author nor the
publisher has received any payment for this "stripped book."

Recycling programs
for this product may
not exist in your area.

ISBN-13: 978-0-373-17555-0
ISBN-10:   0-373-17555-8

HIS MISTLETOE BRIDE

First North American Publication 2008.

Copyright © 2008 by Cara Colter.

All rights reserved. Except for use in any review, the reproduction or
utilization of this work in whole or in part in any form by any electronic,
mechanical or other means, now known or hereafter invented, including
xerography, photocopying and recording, or in any information storage
or retrieval system, is forbidden without the written permission of the
publisher, Harlequin Enterprises Limited, 225 Duncan Mill Road,
Don Mills, Ontario, Canada M3B 3K9.

This is a work of fiction. Names, characters, places and incidents are
either the product of the author's imagination or are used fictitiously,
and any resemblance to actual persons, living or dead, business
establishments, events or locales is entirely coincidental.

This edition published by arrangement with Harlequin Books S.A.

® and TM are trademarks of the publisher. Trademarks indicated with
® are registered in the United States Patent and Trademark Office, the
Canadian Trade Marks Office and in other countries.

www.eHarlequin.com

Printed in U.S.A.

Cara Colter lives on an acreage in British Columbia with her partner, Rob, and eleven horses. She has three grown children and a grandson. She is a recent recipient of a *Romantic Times BOOKreviews* Career Achievement Award in the Love and Laughter category. Cara loves to hear from readers, and you can contact her, or learn more about her, through her Web site at www.cara-colter.com.

Cara Colter brings you
another heartwarming Harlequin Romance®
Hired: Nanny Bride
in May 2009

*Dannie hides a broken heart beneath her
staid nanny uniform. But she wishes gorgeous
entrepreneur Joshua could see the real her. Will this
plain-Jane nanny catch the billionaire playboy's eye?*

To Pat Walls,
a man dedicated to family,
and a true romantic even after forty years!

CHAPTER ONE

OFFICER BRODY TAGGERT decided he was upgrading his mood from cranky to just plain foul.

"As good a time as any to go see Miss L. Toe," he said, out loud, heavy on the sarcasm as he said the name. Tag's dog, Boo, the only other inhabitant of the police cruiser, who was stretched out comfortably in the backseat, woofed what Tag took as agreement.

Actually, Tag thought, given his mood, now was probably not the best time to go see Snow Mountain's newest business owner, resident, budding author and pain in the butt.

Unfortunately the new-in-town Lila Grainger, aka Miss L. Toe, unlike most people Tag ran into who had an alias—an *also known as*—was not a criminal at all. She was the chief of police's niece.

Which was the reason Tag had to go see her.

Directly ordered.

Tag's boss, Chief Paul Hutchinson "Hutch," was notoriously mild-mannered, but he had a core of pure steel and he had not been amused that Tag had missed the first ever meeting of the Save Christmas in Snow Mountain Committee last night.

"She's up to something," the chief had muttered. "She's crafty, just like my sister, her mother. And you missed the meeting, so now we're in the dark."

Tag decided not to point out that *in the* dark was a particularly bad choice of phrase, since that was what had ignited the Christmas fervor in Snow Mountain in the first place.

Town Council had decided to turn off the lights. The Christmas lights, that was. And the traditional Christmas display in the tiny Bandstand Park that was at the end of Main Street was to be no more.

Every year since 1957, the park had been transformed into Santa's Workshop. Ingenious motorized elves made toys and wrapped gifts, reindeer cavorted and Santa ho-ho-hoed and waved. But those particular models of elves and reindeer did not have fifty-year life spans.

Santa's ho-ho-ho had gone into slow mo. Last year one of the elves had seriously overheated and burst into flames. Unfortunately, someone with a cell phone camera had caught on film a child wailing in fear, his face dramatically backlit by the flickering blaze, and Snow Mountain had been put on the map.

The whole issue had been causing heated debates since last January. But at the October Town Council meeting, Leonard Lemoix, who was not Tag's favorite councilor, had gone where no one had gone before. Leonard had crunched the numbers. The cost of the much-needed repairs, setting up, and taking down of the display could, in three years, added up to enough money to buy a new police cruiser.

That didn't even include the cost of the power bill for running the Christmas lights, which were not the new energy-efficient variety, for between six and eight weeks every year.

Town Council had voted unanimously to shut down the

display and Leonard had gone up a notch or two in Tag's estimation.

"My niece thinks it's my fault," the chief had said glumly the day after the meeting. "I didn't know anything about the police cruiser. Now Lila's starting a committee to keep Christmas in Snow Mountain. You know what she said to me? *Uncle Paul, do you want Snow Mountain to be known as the town that canceled Christmas?*"

That's when Tag found out he'd been volunteered to be on the committee.

"We can't have the department looking like villains who want to trade Christmas for a new police cruiser," Hutch said. The chief's increasing concern about *image* seemed to coincide with the arrival of his niece, too.

Lila was a city girl from Miami, and was very savvy about what was and wasn't politically correct.

Despite the fact Tag was developing a dislike for the niece he had not yet met, he knew better than to bother to protest, *why me?* about his appointment to Lila Grainger's committee. After six years on the force he was still, unfortunately, its most recent recruit.

He had shaken the title of rookie, and finally refused to carry the humbling joke badge he'd been required to produce at the whim of anyone senior on the force that said, *Be patient, I'm new here,* but he still got every single assignment that no one else wanted.

Which described the committee to keep Christmas in Snow Mountain to a T. Karl Jamison, the oldest man on the force, kept threatening to retire, which meant there would be a new rookie someday, but not in time, obviously, to save Tag from being at the whim of Hutch's niece.

And now he'd missed her first damned meeting.

Tag had not bothered to offer excuses for his absence at the meeting. He felt his reason for not being there fell into the personal and very private category, and the truth was he would rather face his boss's wrath than his pity. After the death of his younger brother, Ethan, Tag had handled about all the sympathy he could for one lifetime.

Still, he knew now there would be no acceptable excuse— short of an armed robbery in progress—for not going to see Miss L. Toe, aka Lila Grainger, now, tonight, immediately.

Tag swore softly. The dog moaned anxiously, able to detect the downward-spiraling mood in the patrol car.

"It's not your fault, Boo."

The coming of Christmas was not the dog's fault. But with Halloween only a few weeks past, and Thanksgiving not yet here, Tag could have ignored the inevitable coming of the season for a little while longer.

Okay, he'd been *glad* when the town voted against the Christmas display, and not entirely because of the possibility of a new cruiser, either.

In his line of work, Brody Taggert saw the *other* side of Christmas, the side that did not make the front cover of the holiday editions of all the glitzy magazines. He saw what no one ever wanted to acknowledge: the season of joy and faith and miracles had a dirty underbelly, fallout.

As a cop, even a small-town cop, Tag saw firsthand that it was a time of accelerated stress for the people he dealt with most. Soon, after the Thanksgiving turkeys were cleared away, Christmas drinking would begin in earnest. Earnest drinking led to serious trouble: arguments, fights, domestic violence, car accidents, hypothermia, drunken dismantling of business establishments and homes and lives.

This was the conclusion Tag had reached about

Christmas: poor people would feel poorer, lonely people would feel lonelier, desperate people more desperate, mean people meaner.

And of course, anyone who had ever known sorrow, as Tag himself knew sorrow, would feel the ache of that loss all over again, as if it were brand-new. This would be Tag's seventh Christmas without his brother. People had assured him that time would heal his wounds, but this seventh Christmas did not feel any different than the first: bleak, instead of joyous. There was an empty hole in his life that seemed to be made emptier by all the activity and excited anticipation building around him.

But that wasn't Lila Grainger's world.

He'd had a nauseating peek into her world when he'd received her first enthusiastic committee announcement via e-mail three days ago. Animated snowmen danced across a pink background that implored him: Save Christmas In Snow Mountain.

Action Meeting, Free Eggnog And Jeanie Harper's Nearly World Famous Shortbread Cookies.

The dancing snowmen had been particularly irritating to a guy whose computer skills ran to grave satisfaction that he had finally figured out the station's computers were equipped with spelling checkers.

But irritation at the whole concept, and dancing snowmen aside, Tag really had intended to go, and not just because he'd been told it was a good idea, either. The promise of Jeanie's shortbread was more bait than any bachelor could resist, particularly if they were the cookies that she dipped half in chocolate, which they almost always were at this time of year.

But life—real life, not the chocolate-dipped dancing

snowmen variety—had intervened. He sought out his dog in the rearview mirror. Tag had missed the meeting because he'd taken Boo to see a veterinary specialist in Spokane yesterday afternoon.

The truth was he'd been back in plenty of time to make the seven o'clock gathering, but after a man had heard the words, *You'll know when it's time,* he couldn't go. Not didn't want to—couldn't.

Tag was a man who had cleaned up the aftermath of a lot of ugliness, he prided himself on having total control over his emotions. But not even the world's best shortbread cookies could have enticed him off his couch last night. His forty-two-inch flat screen and a hockey game, Boo resting on his lap, had helped him block out his sense of helplessness in the face of the doctor's diagnosis.

Boo was dying. Boo, not just a dog, but a link to his brother; even more than that, a link to life. More than time, it was Boo who had healed in Tag what could be healed.

What Tag hadn't been expecting was how swiftly the chief would react to his absence to Lila's meeting.

He'd been called in to see the chief at the start of his shift, and told he'd better get with the program.

The Save Christmas in Snow Mountain program that was.

Tag was pretty sure if he read over his job description and contract there was nothing in there about having to cooperate with the fruitcake plans of the chief's niece, even if it was going to be good for the police department's image, as Hutch claimed.

The word *image,* up until this point in the department's history, had meant being nice to little kids, keeping a crisp uniform, polished shoes and a clean car and Tag would have been content if it stayed that way forever.

He was also pretty sure there was nothing in his contract about cleaning cells if he didn't comply, either.

On the other hand, Hutch *had* thrown Tag a lifeline, offering him a job on the police department when Tag had just about swamped himself in misery, had been heading down a wrong road *fast,* after Ethan's accident.

The chief had also known, without ever saying one word to indicate that he knew, that he and Boo were partners in the rescue of Tag's troubled soul and so he had turned a blind eye to the dog riding in the backseat. Tag knew he owed Hutch, and owed him dearly.

He turned the patrol car down Main Street. It was just dusk, and the icy winds of mid-November were beginning to blow down Snow Mountain, the black, jagged silhouette forming a backdrop for the town.

Dry leaves and a few newspapers blew down a street lined by single-story brick-and-sandstone businesses that had largely seen a better day. Tilley's Dry Goods had had Going Out Of Business soaped on the windows for at least ten years.

The "D" in the Mountain Drugstore sign was burned out, the odd summertime tourist ventured in there expecting rugs. There were no wintertime tourists, something the optimistic Miss Grainger thought would be a cinch to change.

According to her vibrant pink e-mail, Snow Mountain could not only revive its Christmas display of Santa's Workshop in Bandstand Park, but become a Destination, the capital "D" emphasized with both bold lettering and neon-green.

But as Tag watched the lights winking out, one by one, on Main Street, he thought this was probably the town least likely to ever be a Destination. In fact, he was aware of thinking it wasn't the prettiest picture of small-town U.S.A. that he had ever seen.

He was also aware of missing the garish display of lights and moving figurines in the park at the end of the street just the tiniest little bit.

Lila Grainger's store, of course, was a shining jewel in the middle of that street, the one-hundred-year-old limestone recently sandblasted back to soft, buffed ivory, the new sign hanging above it, green, red and white, saying in tasteful letters, Miss. L. Toe, and in smaller letters underneath it, The Christmas Store At Snow Mountain.

Miss. L. Toe. Cute. Nauseatingly so. Welcome to her world. The opening of the store lent itself to *motive,* too. Lila Grainger had a vested interest in keeping the Christmas in Snow Mountain, now that she'd invested her whole book advance in opening a store here.

When she'd signed a contract to write a book about Christmas, the chief had practically sent out announcement cards he'd been so pleased and proud. Then, unexpectedly, she'd decided to move here from Florida and invest her windfall in this old building.

Tag had yet to meet her, but he had formed a picture of the kind of person who opened a year-round Christmas store on what seemed to be a whim: scrawny, wire-rim glasses, flowered dress, blue eyes spilling over moistly with that do-gooder glow.

The store windows, cleaned until they sparkled, were filled with fairy tale like displays that confirmed his worst suspicions. Mrs. Santa incarnate had arrived in Snow Mountain. One gigantic window display contained an entire town in miniature, completely decked out for Christmas. A train moved through it; he could hear the muffled *choo-choo* of the whistle right through the plate glass.

The other window contained a tree, at least seven feet tall, decorated entirely and in his mind, hideously, in various shades of purple.

It was a fantasy, not appealing at all to a man who spent the days of his life dealing with harsh reality.

"I'm getting a headache," Tag admitted to the dog as he reached over to the seat beside him, put on his hat, pulled the shiny black brim low over his eyes.

The dog whined.

"You are not coming in."

Boo, who usually obeyed instantly and without argument, ignored him, hurtled over the seat into the front of the car and was out the door as soon as Tag opened it.

The dog sat on the sidewalk, and waited, her tail thumping enthusiastically. Tag looked at her, the world's ugliest dog, and felt the downward swoop of his heart.

Cancer. Who knew dogs got cancer?

Boo, the exact color of a mud puddle, had the head of a Great Dane, the body of a Chinese Shar-pei, and the legs of a dachshund. There was nothing the least bit "cute" about the combination of a wrinkled dog with a painfully oversize head waddling around on very crooked and too-short legs.

Tag knew darn well that the visit to the specialist's office, the promise that his Christmases were about to get worse than ever, rather than better, was the real reason his mood was blacker than the silhouette of Snow Mountain. Since he could change nothing, especially not the mood, there was no sense letting it go to waste. The rawness of his own hurt was under control tonight, as it had not been last night.

He felt a moment's sympathy for Miss L. Toe, having to face him when he was in this frame of mind, but then he quelled it.

He debated wrestling Boo back into the car, but the dog had an amazing instinct for people: Boo could tell good from bad with such telepathic accuracy it was spooky. Even before the dog saw a person, while Tag was still sitting in his cruiser running a license plate, Boo would be watching intently, sniffing the air, "sensing" things unseen.

The truth was people, even ones as cynical as Tag, could be fooled.

They could be fooled by a pretty face or an angelic air, by white hair and granny glasses, by adolescent awkwardness, by words, by body language.

Not Boo. The hackles on the dog's neck rose when something—or someone—needed a second look, and she grinned the silliest grin when everything was all right. Tag did not substitute her judgment for his own, but the world's ugliest dog had an uncanny knack for letting him know when he'd missed something.

She wasn't officially a K-9, but she was unofficially the mascot of the Snow Mountain Police Department.

So, why not see how she would react to the chief's niece? Just for interest's sake, nothing more. Lila Grainger's appearance and the opening of her store seemed mysterious and sudden, as if Tag needed to be any warier than he was of the woman he had never even laid eyes on. Still, the chief was usually a talker—you couldn't shut him up when she'd signed the book deal—but he'd said nothing about his niece's arrival in town until she had gotten here.

Tag ignored the big No Dogs Allowed sign posted on

the door, since just about everyone in Snow Mountain knew Boo was more human than dog anyway, and pulled the brass handle on the heavy walnut and glass door. He stepped in. A sleigh bell jingled a greeting and he was enveloped by smells of Christmas: candy cane, mint, pumpkin pie, incense, spices, pine.

Scent, he had found, was the most powerful of triggers and the aromas swamped him in memories of what his life had once felt like and had once been. A longing for the sweet, uncomplicated days of the past enveloped him. For a moment he could almost see his brother, Ethan, at about age six, tearing into a train set not unlike that one that chugged around the window.

He shook off the feeling of melancholy, liking crankiness better. A carol played loudly, old school Bing Crosby, and everywhere he looked Tag saw the highly breakable paraphernalia of the season. He warned Boo, with a finger, not to move.

At the far end of the store, a slight figure sat behind a counter had her back to the door and was typing furiously. She had not heard him come in over the high-volume crooning of Bing and her own intensity, and he studied her, frowning. No flowered dress?

In fact, the woman seemed to be wearing low-rider jeans that were slipping to show quite a bit of naked and very slender lower back. Tendrils of blond hair, the color of fall grass streaked with liquid honey, had escaped a clasp and teased the top of a delicate neck.

Tag's first thought was that it couldn't be the chief's niece. Hutch had a town full of relatives, not a niece or nephew under forty. This girl looked like she was about eighteen.

The wind picked that moment to send a vicious gust

down Main Street, and it sucked the door out of his hand and slammed it so hard even the dog flinched.

The woman, who had just reached for her coffee mug, started, and the glass dropped from fingers that had not quite grasped it, and shattered on the newly refurbished hardwood floor.

She leaped from the chair, and whirled to face him, one hand over her heart, the other reaching frantically for the three-foot-high striped candy cane decoration in a box beside her.

She held it like a weapon, and he might have laughed at what a ridiculous defense a candy cane was, except that somehow the picture of his brother ripping into Christmas parcels was still with him, as was his agony over Boo, and his laughter felt as dried up as those fall leaves blowing down Main Street.

Miss Mary Christmas was not eighteen after all, but midtwenties maybe.

And her eyes were genuinely fear-glazed, in sharp contrast to the pretty joy and light world she had created in her store. She registered his uniform and her hold on the candy cane relaxed, but only marginally.

She was dressed casually, but her outfit showed off feminine curves so appealing it pierced the armor of his hurt, which made him frown. She wore hip-hugging jeans, a red sweater over a white shirt, the tails and collar sticking out. She was sock-footed, which for some reason took him off guard, an intimacy at odds with the store surroundings.

"Sorry," she said, "you startled me."

No kidding.

He glanced down at Boo who did something he had never seen before: laid down and began to hum, deep in her throat, not a growl, a strange lullaby. He stared at the dog, flummoxed, hoping this was not the next stage in the diagnosis the doctor had given him yesterday.

He looked back up, as confused by her as he had been by the dog's strange humming.

She was young and beautiful, like one of those angels they sold to top the Christmas tree. Her Florida skin was only faintly sun-kissed, flawless as porcelain, her bone structure was gorgeous, but fragile, and eyes huge and china-blue fastened on his face. He could see where her pulse still beat frantically in her neck.

"You must be Miss Grainger," he said, despite the fact he'd been determined to address her as Miss L. Toe. Now he was aware of keeping his voice deliberately soft, his reasons for being here, nebulous to begin with, even more blurred by the fear he saw in her.

"Lila," she insisted brightly.

The chief's niece did not have the chunky build of the rest of the Hutchinson clan. In fact, he was aware of feeling guilty even thinking it about the chief's niece, but she was subtly but undeniably, well, *sexy.*

She was trying to make it look like she wasn't afraid anymore, but he could tell she still was, so he tried to tame his frown, and canned his plans to take out his bad mood on her.

He was in a business where he got thrown plenty of curve-balls, but he had never developed a liking for being caught off guard, surprised, and the chief's niece was a surprise.

He'd been around enough fear to recognize the real McCoy, and to see wariness still haunted her eyes, despite his uniform. Or maybe because of it. Lots of people were afraid of police. He kept the space between them, but Boo began to wiggle forward on her belly, still humming happily. Tag snapped his finger at his dog, pointed at his feet.

Boo gave him a pleading look over her shoulder, then flopped over on her back and pointed all four feet in the air.

Lila Grainger's eyes left his face for the first time. Despite his uniform, he had the feeling she would bolt for the back if he made one move toward her. But when she looked at Boo, she smiled, and some finely held tension left her.

"What an adorable dog."

Maybe that explained her overreaction to the slamming of the door. Visual impairment. Boo was about the furthest thing from adorable on the planet!

An upside-down paw waved at her, and Lila Grainger laughed, proving she could see just fine, and that she was even sexier than he had first thought, which was unfortunate, because he'd rated her plenty sexy on that first glance.

"I missed the meeting last night," Tag said, getting down to business. He folded his arms over his chest, to make himself look big and remote, not a man in the least moved by the sexiness of strangers.

"Meeting?" she stammered, uneasily.

"I've been assigned to the Committee." He wanted to make that very plain. Assigned. Not volunteered.

"Oh, *that* meeting," she said too hastily, and tucked a wisp of that feathery hair behind her ear, "That's fine. We have enough people. More than enough. You look like a busy guy. No time for this type of thing. But thanks for dropping by. There's some leftover shortbread by the cash register. Go ahead and take some."

She was *trying* to get rid of him. Even with the distraction of the cookies, which he stole a glance at and saw *were* chocolate dipped, and with the further distraction of that wisp of hair popping back out from behind her ear, the policeman in him went on red alert as her eyes shifted uneasily to the right. The chief had been right. She was up to something. Something that she didn't want him to know about.

He was really watching her now. Every detail suddenly interested him, including ones that had nothing to do with what she might be trying to hide, like the fact she had faint circles under her eyes, as if she had trouble sleeping, and the fact that her ring finger was empty.

She was single. Miss L. Toe not Mrs. L. Toe. There was absolutely no reason he should feel uneasy about that. He didn't do the relationship thing. He'd become a master at ignoring that initial twitch of interest that could lead a man into that quicksand world of caring.

At his brother's funeral, six and a half years ago, the minister had said, *All love leads to loss.* Somehow it had become a credo Tag lived by—the dog had wormed her way by his defenses, but no one else.

And now, Boo, too, was going to drive the point home. That to develop attachments, to care about anything, even a dog, made a man vulnerable, stole his power from him as surely as Delilah had stolen Sampson's hair.

Not that he could indulge in such introspection right now. He made himself not look at Boo, who was still waving her paw engagingly at Lila Grainger.

"Well, nice of you to drop in, Officer, um—"

"Taggert," he supplied. What was causing her to feel such discomfort? He'd startled her, but there was more. He could sense it, even without Boo's help. Her uncle had been absolutely right.

She was up to something.

Or else the news he'd gotten yesterday, and that sudden poignant memory of his brother tearing into that gift, had rattled him badly enough that he was jumping at shadows.

After all, what could she be up to that she wouldn't want the police department—her uncle—to know about? She hardly looked like the type to decide to finance the saving of Christmas with a little illegal activity, like selling drugs or smuggling.

Still, Tag had a cop's gift. He knew instinctively when people were hiding something, and she was.

"Have you got some minutes from the meeting?" he pushed, just a little.

"Minutes?" her voice became suspiciously squeaky. "Of course not. It was very informal."

"So did you come up with a plan of action? For saving the Christmas display in Bandstand Park?"

"Oh," Lila said, her voice filled with bright and very fake cheer again, "we just bounced some preliminary ideas around. You know."

"I don't," he said uncooperatively.

"We changed the name. We're going to call ourselves Save Our Snow Mountain Christmas. SOS for short."

She looked at him like she expected his approval. When he said nothing she began to talk fast and nervously, another sure sign of a person who was being evasive.

"We might put up a tree. A big one," she said in a rush, "just to keep the Christmas spirit alive until we can come up with some money and get the Santa's Workshop display fixed. Or get the town to change their minds."

She blushed when she said that, as if she was planning

something *naughty* to get the town to change their minds, but just looking at her he could tell her idea of naughty and his would be completely different. He thought if she showed up in one of those red, fur-trimmed bikinis the town would do whatever the hell she wanted.

As if to prove how differently their minds worked, and that she was the girl least likely to ever wear a red fur-trimmed bikini, she said, "We might try putting a real Santa in the park on weekends."

"There are no real Santas," he said dryly, knowing with new conviction he was hearing only part of the story.

"I was thinking of asking that portly man who works with Uncle Paul. Do you think he'd do it for free?"

Portly was a very kind way to describe the most senior member of the Snow Mountain department.

"Jamison?" Tag asked, incredulously. "You want Karl Jamison to play Santa?"

Jamison, who was not portly, but obese, who chewed—and spat—tobacco, and who had the world's largest off-color vocabulary thanks to ten years in the Marine Corp, was the man least likely to play Santa.

"He just looked like he'd make a good Santa," she said wistfully.

Karl Jamison was the man most likely to kill Christmas forever on Snow Mountain should he ever be appointed a weekend Santa Claus.

"You wouldn't make a good Santa," she said, eyeing Tag speculatively before turning her eyes away, fiddling with the candy cane. "You're too—"

Despite the insult of being declared a worse Santa than Jamison, a number of ways to finish that sentence came to his mind: tall, dark, handsome, which just served to prove he had not been as successful at shutting down that initial spark of interest as he had hoped.

But she shot him another glance and finished her sentence with, "Unjolly."

He was not a literary giant like her, but he was pretty sure if he ran unjolly through the computer spelling checker at the station, it was going to make that noise he hated.

Still, *unjolly* was as accurate a description as any, so why was he vaguely annoyed that she had spotted his true nature, completely unsuitable in the peace and joy department, so instantly and accurately?

And since she had handed him his escape from her ridiculous committee practically gift-wrapped, why wasn't he gratefully bowing his way toward the door?

Instead he heard himself asking, "So besides that, did you come up with any other ideas for saving Christmas in Snow Mountain?"

He did not try to hide his cynicism, and her look of uneasiness increased.

"No, nothing at all," she said, way, way too quickly.

She was afraid of *him*. Or something. There were a lot of mysteries in Lila Grainger's eyes, and a man could be drawn to them, tempted to probe them, which was another reason to just get out of here, accept with grace and gratitude there was no room for cynical, Christmas-hating cops on the SOS committee.

But the chief wasn't going to believe he hadn't done something: kicked an elf, broken a manger, been rude and unreasonable, to get himself off the Save Christmas Committee hook. He slid one wistful look over his shoulder at the door, but sucked it up.

"You're sure you don't want me to do something?" he

asked gruffly. Damn. Now he was probably going to end up building a Santa throne that could hold Jamison without collapsing. Which would be a gigantic project.

But she was as eager to get rid of him as he was to leave.

"No, really, I can't think of a single thing." In fact, now she was backing away from him.

Only she'd forgotten the broken glass on the floor, and she was in her socks. She cried out, lifted her foot, the heel already crimson with blood.

"It's nothing," she said as he moved instinctively toward her. She slammed her foot back down with such conviction she nearly made herself faint.

She toppled, just as he arrived at her, and he managed to scoop her up before she hit the floor. She weighed practically nothing, perhaps a few pounds more than Boo, not that she was anything like Boo.

It had been a long, long time since he had held anything so close and so soft as Miss Lila Grainger. A yearning so intense it nearly stole his breath shot through him. Before he could stop himself, he had pulled her scent, wild summer strawberries, deep inside himself and it felt as if it was filling an emptiness he had not thought could be filled.

He wanted to drop her. He wanted to hold her tighter. He wanted to be the same man he had been thirty seconds ago, and was not sure he ever could be again.

"Oh, my," she moaned, her breath warm against his chest. "This has gone very badly."

He felt her sweet weight in her arms, saw the pulse going crazy in her neck, heard the dog humming at his heel with what he could suddenly and clearly identify as adoration, and thought, *You got that right.*

Out loud he said, without a single shred of emotion that might clue her in to how he felt about her softness pressed against him, "Where's your first-aid kit?"

CHAPTER TWO

LILA sat on the edge of the toilet in the bathroom, staring at the dark head bent over her foot.

Despite the fact Officer Taggert had perfected that policeman look of professional remoteness, he had actually flinched at the bathroom decor, which she knew to be fabulous: an imaginative creation of what Santa's washroom would look like.

There was a fake window, framed in snowmen-patterned curtains, looking out over beautifully hand-painted scenes from the North Pole. The towels had Christmas trees on them, the soap had glitter, the toilet paper, one of her top selling items, was printed with Ho, Ho, Ho.

In fact, before he had arrived, Lila had been sitting at her desk, contemplating starting her first ever book, *How to Have a Perfect Christmas,* with a really fun chapter on bathroom decorating for the holidays.

But now, despite the cheer of the bright red and white paint and the merry decor, the atmosphere in the close quarters of the bathroom seemed mildly icy. Taggert was remote, determined to keep his professional distance though, really, it seemed a little too late for that.

She had already *felt* him, felt the hard, unrelenting,

pure-man strength of him, and been as dazed by that as by the pain in her foot.

Dazed would describe her reaction to him, period—the reason she had stepped on broken glass.

After the initial fear had come something even more frightening. A feeling, unfounded because you could not *know* a person from simply looking at them.

But her feeling had been instant, and felt deeply.

The world is a better place because this man is in it.

She tried to thrust the thought away as soon as she had it. You could not know that about a complete stranger, even if he was wearing a police uniform. Despite making great strides since arriving in Snow Mountain, she was not sleeping well, and she knew her judgment was not what it once had been.

Naturally, now, she was doing her darnedest to be as perfectly poised and professional as he was, trying to act as though being picked up and carried down the hall by an extraordinarily appealing man was an everyday ho-hum kind of experience for her.

The dog seemed determined for them all to get cozy again. It had squeezed in between the toilet bowl and the sink, and was nuzzling her hand with its warm, damp nose.

"This really isn't necessary," she said again, her *world is a better place* feeling causing her to feel guilty about the secret she was determined to keep from him.

She was amazed that he had not seen the results of last night's meeting crammed into the dark corner by the bathroom: protest signs, freshly painted.

Lila had found out this morning that it was necessary to have a permit to assemble in Snow Mountain, a ridiculous formality given the tininess of the town, she felt. She had also found out that it took a number of weeks to get a permit, and she needed to draw attention to the fact Town Council had voted to cancel Christmas at Snow Mountain, *now.*

The unpermitted protest was scheduled for the Thursday before Thanksgiving. The SOS team was nearly delirious with delight over the plan to close down Main Street right in front of the town hall until some funding was reinstated for the Santa's Workshop display at Bandstand Park.

Her committee was not a bunch of hotheaded rebels, either, not the kind of people one would ordinarily expect at a protest. They were nice people, decent, law-abiding, hardworking people who were willing to stand up for what they believed in.

And they believed in Christmas.

Still, Lila was pretty sure her uncle would kill her if he knew. And this man in front of her? If the world *was* a better place because of him, it was probably because he would be exceedingly intolerant of schemes that fell even the *teensiest* bit outside of the law.

She shivered, still taken totally aback by her reaction of such total awareness to Officer Taggert. She, of all people, knew to be distrustful of instant attraction, since she had paid the horrific price of someone's totally unwanted and unencouraged attraction to her.

She'd been reminded of the consequences of that just a few minutes ago, when she'd once again experienced that horrible startled reflex, a reflex she had assured herself was almost gone—until the door had slammed tonight.

She had known as soon as she'd arrived in Snow Mountain that her doubts about opening the first storefront for her unexpectedly successful Internet Christmas company had been unfounded. It had been the right decision to pack up her life and move across the country.

Her healing, her return to normal, could begin here, in this sleepy little town nestled among forests and mountains.

Finally she was going to be able to overcome the block that she'd been experiencing ever since she'd been approached, because of the Internet success of her small company, to write *How to Have a Perfect Christmas* under the pseudonym, Miss L. Toe.

For weeks now, Lila had been experiencing excitement and hope instead of that horrible feeling of flatness, interspersed with anxiety. Except for the sleep problem, she was feeling so much better.

Snow Mountain had so much unrealized potential! It was a magical place, a town off a Christmas card. It was the place that could inspire her to write a *great* first book, to launch a *great* storefront for her Internet business.

But no lights? No Christmas display in the town square?

She remembered that display so clearly from the time her family had flown up here from their home in Florida to spend Christmas with her mother's oldest brother, Uncle Paul, the year she'd turned ten. She still remembered that Christmas more vividly than any other. The magic of snow, and real Christmas trees, the feeling in that small town.

Maybe that's what had pulled her back to this place when her world had fallen apart.

So, she just wasn't having Town Council squash her dreams before they even got started! She was giving herself over to creating the perfect Christmas store and the perfect Christmas town and the perfect book on creating the perfect Christmas. It gave her a sense of safety and control over the things that had been snatched from her.

Her arrival in Snow Mountain had returned to her a belief that there were places in the world that were wonderfully old-fashioned, where children still walked to school and played in the streets without their parents hovering, where women never gave a thought to walking alone, where violent things rarely happened.

But then the wrench—Town Council practically canceling Christmas!

Still, despite that challenge to her control over creating the perfect Christmas, Lila was aware of beginning to feel safe again. Tonight was a perfect example: She'd left her door unlocked even after store hours.

Lila was aware that her initial reaction of panic to the unexpected arrival in her shop had faded. It had not faded because she knew the man who had changed her world forever was in jail, but rather illogically because Officer Taggert radiated the strength and calm—the certain forbidding sternness—of a man who could be relied on to protect, to keep the world safe, to uphold standards of decency.

At first, she'd felt anxious that maybe he'd heard a whisper about the planned protest, especially when he seemed so suspicious, *probing*. Minutes of the meeting, for Pete's sake.

But it had soon become very apparent to her that, despite his offer to help, Officer Taggert's heart was not in it *at all*. He'd been ordered here by her uncle, and had put in an appearance.

Unless he saw the signs on his way out the door, the protest was safe.

She felt the tiniest little shiver of apprehension that she was on the wrong side of the law, but her purpose was so *right* that she felt justified.

Then it occurred to her that maybe the shiver she was feeling was not apprehension, but a treacherous little stirring of something else, despite the deliberate remoteness of the man who shared the bathroom with her.

Appreciation, primal compared to her rather philosophical thought that the world was a better place because he was in it. It was an almost clinical awareness of a healthy female for a healthy male. It didn't help that she had felt the strong bands of his arms around her, his easy strength as he had carried her to the bathroom.

He had seemed indifferent to their close proximity. But then again, he'd missed the protest signs, and he didn't look like a man who missed much, so maybe he'd felt a forbidden little stirring, too. He was a healthy male after all.

Taggert was at least six-one of pure male perfection: sleek muscle, long legs, deep chest, broad, broad shoulders, all accentuated magnificently by the crisp lines of his light blue on navy police uniform.

His face was astounding, chiseled masculine perfection, unconscious strength in the set of his chin, the firmness around his mouth, the lines around his eyes. His eyes, which had initially been shaded by the brim of his hat, were now fully visible since he had removed the hat.

While the rest of him was pure cop, one-hundred-percent intimidating and authoritative presence, his eyes were the softest shade of brown, shot through with threads of pure gold. His eyes did not reflect the remoteness of his demeanor, though there were walls up in them, walls that guarded a mystery…and most likely his heart.

He carried himself with the utter confidence of a man who knew his own strength and capabilities perfectly. No swagger, only pure, unadulterated self-assurance.

Now he was on one knee in front of her, focused on her foot. His hair was short, but incredibly thick and shiny, the rich color of dark chocolate. She was amazed by a renegade desire to feel its silk beneath her fingertips.

His hands were unbelievably sure on her ankle, and she stifled a gasp when he pulled her sock away and held her naked foot in the warm, hard cup of his hand. The shiver of appreciation she'd felt graduated to a betraying tingle of pure awareness. She felt terrified in a much different way than she had felt terrified the last two years of her life when she had become the victim of a stalker. He was a man she had worked with, and whose interest in her had seemed so benign…at first.

"Really," she managed to croak, "I can look after it."

"Look, either I'm taking a look at it, or I'm taking you to the hospital. You choose."

He glanced up, and she noticed just the faintest shadow of whiskers on his clean-shaven face, felt swamped by his closeness, his pure masculine scent.

"Are you all right?" he asked, genuine concern faintly overriding the professionalism in the masculine deepness of his voice. "You aren't going to faint, are you?"

"Faint?" she managed to say, inserting proud outrage into her voice, a woman determined not to be seen as weak ever again. "I am not the fainting kind."

But she had managed to sound more certain than she actually felt. Was she all right? Why did she feel as if she was standing in the open doorway of a plane, deciding whether to jump?

"I've been doing this a long time," he said patiently. "There is no fainting *kind.* I've seen a Marine faint at the sight of his own blood."

"Oh."

"Can I go ahead then? Or do you want me to take you to the hospital?"

The eyes were intent on her face, the voice no-nonsense, though his offering her a choice relaxed something in her, even though, logically, she knew it was not a *real* choice and he was very much in control.

"Go ahead," she squeaked.

"It's not so bad," he reassured her, lifting her leg so he could get a good look at the heel, gently swabbing away the blood with an alcohol pad. "I see a single cut, not very deep. I think there's a little piece of glass still in there."

He reached for tweezers, tugged, held up a tiny fragment of glass for her to see before he dropped it into the waste-paper basket that was painted like a toy drum.

"I'm just going to dress the wound," he explained, his voice deep, soothing, as if he was talking to a small child. "I don't see any more glass, no need for stitches. A wound to this part of the body just bleeds a lot."

The voice of a man who had seen many wounds and much blood, without ever coming even remotely close to fainting; a man who would be just this coolly and reassuringly competent in crises of any magnitude.

He placed a cotton gauze on her foot, held it in place by winding a bandage over her heel and up her ankle in a criss-cross pattern, all very professional, clinical, detached.

Not, apparently, being bothered by *tingles* the way she was.

"You're obviously used to doing this sort of thing," she said. "This is obviously your first trip to the North Pole, though."

He looked surprised, and then he smiled.

It was just the tiniest hint of a smile, but it changed the stern lines of his face completely. She glimpsed for a moment something of his past: something reckless, devil-may-care, mischievous. *Charming.*

He got up, picked up his hat and brushed off his knee with it. He glanced around at the bathroom decor, his eyes resting briefly on a jar of bright candies labeled Jolly Beans, For Medicinal Use Only.

The smile that had tickled his lips evaporated, and she was aware whatever he had once been, he was not that now. He actually winced, as if such adorable corniness hurt his eyes. He stepped quickly out of the bathroom and back into the hallway.

All she could think of was he had nearly brushed against the protest signs, and for the first time in her life she was completely unworthy of trust.

He clamped his hat back on his head, pulled it low, so his amazing eyes were once more shadowed. Then he whistled for his dog, and let himself out the front door.

She limped after him and locked it behind him, aware that even though Snow Mountain itself felt safer to her than it had half an hour ago, she herself did not feel as safe, as if she stood on the edge of something scary. And wonderful.

But that she of all people, she reminded herself with stern warning, should know how very scary a brief encounter with a strange man could become.

It was the reason she'd sworn off real life and chosen to embrace fantasy instead. Her beautiful store, this beautiful town, her literary adventures—those were going to be enough for her. It was going to fill every void, make her feel safe, fulfilled, *in control.*

A woman would never feel one hundred percent in control around a man like Taggert. Never.

Determined to make the creation of a perfect Christmas her life mission, she marched back to her computer.

Suddenly decorating a bathroom seemed like a terrible place to start *How to Have A Perfect Christmas*. Terrible.

"You have to start somewhere," she told herself, aware of a panicky little edge in her voice as she said it. She'd accepted the advance, and worse, she'd *spent* it. She had a deadline!

Obviously the writer's block was coming, at least in part, from her insomnia. But it wasn't helping one little bit that the place on earth most likely to be chosen for a poster of the perfect Christmas town had practically canceled Christmas. Once she looked after that, everything else was going to fall into place.

With a new sense of verve, Lila picked up the phone, took a deep breath and did the thing she had been debating about and putting off since the meeting last night.

"CLEM TV, Spokane," a voice on the other end answered.

"Could I speak to Jade Flynn, please?" She named the reporter who seemed to do the majority of the human interest stories for the station.

"Can I tell her what you're calling about?"

"The cancellation of Christmas," Lila said firmly.

Brody Taggert joined the other men at the window of the Snow Mountain Police Department, took a sip of his coffee and looked across Main Street at the fracas outside of Snow Mountain Town Hall.

The protesters had completely blocked the street, and were enthusiastically waving lovingly hand-painted signs.

Elves Have Rights, Too! Say Yes To Christmas. Save Our Snow Mountain. Save Santa. As they marched around in a circle, they chanted, "Heck no, the elves won't go."

It was an unlikely-looking group of protestors—not a dreadlock or pierced body part on any of them. Lots of gray hair out there, with one glaring exception, of course.

Her hair, where it showed beneath the brim of her fur-trimmed Santa hat, was catching the sun, and looked like it was spun through with gold.

It seemed to him Lila Grainger was as eye-catching in that hat, bundled up in a pink oversize parka that made her look like a marshmallow, as she would have been in a fur-trimmed bikini.

The CLEM TV mobile van from Spokane was pulling up. Bruce Wilkes from the *Snow Mountain News* was already happily snapping pictures.

"What are you going to do, Chief?" Randy Mulligan asked uncertainly.

Tag slid Hutch a look. *Have a heart attack,* came to mind. The chief looked apoplectic.

Of course, his niece, looking positively radiant, was in the very middle of the mêlée. When she separated from the other protestors to go and talk to Jade Flynn, who was getting out of the news van, it was more than obvious who was in charge of the protest.

Tag, instead of making the professional assessment *ringleader,* noticed that aside from the fact she looked cute as a button, she was still limping.

"You didn't even catch a whisper of this when you went to see her?" Hutch asked Tag accusingly.

"No, sir. She told me they were going to ask Jamison to play Santa—"

"Like hell I'm playing Santa," Jamison muttered indignantly, putting enough curse words between playing and Santa to do his Marine corps heritage proud.

"—and that they'd come up with a new name. That's it." Well, that wasn't it. Tag had known she was up to something *naughty*. He could now clearly remember the *guilty* blush when she'd mentioned getting city hall to change their minds. He felt he'd probably been distracted by *naughty* thoughts of his own, especially after he'd carried her down that endless hall to her bathroom, and then spent agonizing minutes administering first-aid to the cut on her foot.

You didn't admit to your boss you'd had naughty thoughts about his niece, thoughts that might have prevented you from seeing certain things coming, he told himself.

Besides, the grim news about Boo had been pretty fresh that night; Tag knew it had clouded his thinking, and still did, though he wore the mask of functioning perfectly.

"Go arrest her," Hutch said, thankfully to no one in particular.

Randy Mulligan obviously thought of some urgent work he had to do. He stampeded from the room as if the Hells Angels had arrived in town and he had to personally deal with them.

"Arrest her?" Pete Harper said. "Are you kidding? You know how that's going to look on the evening news? This town has barely recovered from the elf on fire last year."

"How's it going to look if I don't arrest her and she's my niece?" Hutch snapped. "Like I'm playing favorites, that's how. If I don't do something decisive right now every special interest group in Snow Mountain from the Grannies for Justice to Pals for Pooches is going to think they can shut down the town anytime they don't get what they want.

Pals for Pooches has been trying to get an animal shelter for a lot longer than Lila's been trying to save Christmas."

Unfortunately Tag could see his point.

"Well, I'm not arresting her," Pete said. "My mother would kill me."

His mother was out there right beside Lila, carrying a sign that showed a tombstone with Santa on it, RIP, and then Killed By Snow Mountain Town Council. Jeanie Harper was also dispensing cookies to the news crews, practically guaranteeing all stories would be slanted in favor of the protestors.

As if they wouldn't be anyway.

"I ain't arresting nobody, either," Jamison said. He jerked his thumb at Pete. "His mother wouldn't bake me cookies anymore."

Pete shot him a look. "My mother bakes *you* cookies?"

"Go arrest her, Tag," Hutch said wearily.

It fell neatly into that category of a job no one else wanted to do, and besides, he was the one who had missed the signs that this was going to happen. Now that he thought about it, hadn't there been something stuffed in that dark corner of the hallway by her bathroom?

Oh, yeah, signs.

"You mean arrest her?" Tag hedged uncomfortably, "Or just take her aside, and try to talk some sense into her?"

Her uncle sighed. "She's just like her mother. Talking sense to her is like trying to explain algebra to a chimp. Impossible. Besides, you think she's going to give in quietly? What kind of news story would that make?"

Unfortunately Tag could see his point. He took a deep breath, squared his shoulders, turned and lifted his jacket off the back of his chair, pulled on his hat. Boo, who had been snoozing under his desk, lifted her head and thumped her tail on the floor, hopeful for an invitation.

"Fat chance," he told her sourly, while silently searching for signs of the dog's deterioration. "I count on you to warn me about who I have to keep an eye on. You failed me on this one, Boo. You *loved* Lila Grainger."

He realized he did not want to be using the word love in any sentence addressed to Boo, especially one that also included the name Lila Grainger. She was just that kind of woman, the kind who could storm a man's defenses before he even knew he was under attack.

The kind of woman where you noticed the fact she was limping, rather than the fact she was leading an insurrection.

The kind of woman with a foot so enchanting, you overlooked the signs of revolt brewing all around you.

The dog sighed, put her head back down and closed her eyes. Almost easier to go out there and deal with *that* than the dog's easy surrender to being left behind.

Moments later, he was shouldering his way through a crowd worthy of a big-city Santa Claus parade, with the same attitude of excited anticipation in the air. There hadn't been this much excitement in Snow Mountain since the Snow Leopards, the high school football team, had made state finals three years ago.

Over the chanting, Tag could hear a tinny loudspeaker wailing out a sentimental rendition of the song, "You Light up My Life."

It seemed as if the entire population of Snow Mountain—plus most of the surrounding area—had known about the demonstration. This was a town that could not keep secrets, so how it had stayed below the police radar was something of a miracle.

The air of celebration toned down a bit as he shoved his way through to the center of activity. He tried to tell himself he had probably been in worse positions, but he could not remember when.

By the time he arrived in front of Lila Grainger, he was very aware of the hostility the crowd had toward him.

She saw him coming. So did the news crews. Every camera, cell phone and video recorder within a hundred miles had accumulated in front of town hall. And every single one of them was pointed at him.

"Hello, Officer Taggert," she said bravely, trying for, but missing, defiance. Hell, she was trembling slightly.

"Miss Grainger."

Damn it. She looked adorable in the ridiculous hat. The oversize coat made her look even smaller than she was.

He leaned close to her, could smell that heady scent of wild strawberries, tried to avoid the mistake he had made last time of breathing in too much of it. He fought back a sudden impulse to ask her about her damned foot. "Miss Grainger, would you come with me?"

He said it quietly, for her ears only. She looked like the type that buckled under to authority, but of course the wild-strawberry scent should have warned him of, well, a wilder side.

She took a step back from him, fixed the incredible deep sea-blue of her eyes on him, and squared her shoulders. "Am I under arrest, Officer Taggert?"

Jeanie Harper gasped, which probably meant a life sentence of no more shortbread for Tag, her son or Jamison. This was not something he wanted to be held responsible for, but he was the new guy. The flak always landed on him.

The cameras were snapping, the film rolling. The news crew moved in closer, and Jade Flynn flipped her hair and moistened her lips, her timing for the story impeccable. Microphones shaped like huge foam hot dogs dangled over them.

"You need a permit to assemble," he said quietly. "You're obstructing traffic."

"Am I under arrest?" she demanded again. She pointed her chin upward, stubbornly, but he could see she was shaking even more now.

And that she was all of five foot three and probably weighed about a hundred and ten pounds. He remembered that weight in his arms, struggled to keep his facial expression absolutely impassive.

Standing there in her Santa hat, she looked exactly like the girl who had probably not done one *naughty* thing in her whole life. She'd probably never even had a speeding ticket, never mind fur-trimmed bikinis.

She was just one of those people who became passionate about causes. Not that he wanted to be thinking about *her* and *passion*. What a waste. All that passion over a silly display in the park.

Though every time he drove by Bandstand Park, he had to admit he was aware of the black emptiness of it, instead of the lights, the little characters, Santa's reverberating ho-ho-ho. Suddenly, without warning, he remembered Ethan coming home when he was about twelve with Santa's hat, swiped from the park.

And he, the older brother, making him take it back, foreshadowing his career, which at this moment he hated.

"Are you arresting me, Officer Taggert?"

"Yeah," he said reluctantly, "you're under arrest."

A discontented hum began in the crowd. Jeanie called out, "Shame on you, Brody Taggert."

This was the problem with becoming a police officer in the small town where you had grown up. Jeanie Harper no doubt had memories of him raiding her garden, and knocking over her mailbox on Halloweens past.

He put a hand on Lila's shoulder, intending to guide her out of the crowd, but she shrugged out from under his hand, and stubbornly presented her wrists to him.

He bit the inside of his cheek, whether to keep his temper or to keep from laughing he wasn't quite sure. Miss L. Toe did look ludicrous, but since he had not laughed since Boo's diagnosis, he figured it was his temper.

He heard Jade Flynn say to her cameraman, "Oh, boy. Be sure and get this."

Everybody wanted a show to go with the storyline about the town that was canceling Christmas. And every show needed a villain. Jade Flynn didn't care who looked bad. Lila looked like she might, but not enough to let go of this opportunity to get the publicity she wanted.

And he was the *who* that was going to look bad.

He stared her down, she was obviously frightened, but not enough to back down. She was willing to sacrifice herself to her cause. He noticed she still had little circles of fatigue under her eyes.

"Okay then," he said, his voice deliberately flat, his expression hard. "Put your hands behind your back."

She did and he took the cuffs off his belt, and snapped them around her wrists, which were so small he had to adjust the cuffs. He was nearly blinded by flashes, and he felt like an idiot. If she was humiliated it didn't show one little bit in the proud tilt of her chin.

He told her she was being arrested for unlawful assembly and obstructing traffic, and told her her rights. She nodded that she understood, standing ramrod straight, her dignity intact while he felt his own was in tatters.

He spun her around, his hand on her elbow and marched her, her limp visible, through the crowd. He was aware of feeling as if he had to protect her from the crush of people, though it was him getting the looks. Several people clicked their heels and gave him straight-armed salutes.

Lila flinched more than he did from the insulting gestures.

As soon as he had his prisoner safely inside the police station, Hutch appeared.

"Was that really necessary?" he asked Tag of the cuffs.

Tag said nothing, but sighed inwardly. Who had ordered the arrest? Still, he was now aware this was something of a family dispute. No one ever wanted to be in the middle of *that.*

"Ask her," Tag said, and unlocked her wrists.

"He was just doing his job, Uncle Paul."

Tag shot her a look that clearly told her he didn't need a one-hundred-pound waif in a Santa hat and a marshmallow coat to defend him.

"Get into my office," Hutch said quietly to his niece. "Now."

She sent Tag an imploring look, which he ignored. He'd done his bit, and he wasn't the least bit proud of it, either.

"I'm not normally the kind of person who gets arrested," Lila said to him, ignoring her uncle's command, the only person Tag had ever seen do that.

"I kind of figured you for a virgin," he said, their department's lingo for a first-time offender.

It had slipped out, and it was a mistake. He knew it even before Hutch sent him a killing look and her blush went the color of a smashed raspberry.

Which of course made him entertain the extremely

naughty thought that maybe she was every kind of virgin it was possible to be.

"Sorry," he muttered. "I didn't mean that the way it sounded."

"Of course not," she said soothingly. "We're all rattled."

The thing was, he *shouldn't* be. He was no virgin. Of any kind.

"I hope we meet again," she said formally, "under better circumstances."

"Really? I was hoping the exact opposite." He knew as soon as he said it, it was way too harsh, a defense against everything she was making him *feel*. Rattled. Off-kilter. Guilty. Worried about her foot.

Boo chose that moment to waddle out from under his desk. She plopped down at Lila's feet and began humming.

Lila sat down on the floor beside the dog, wrapped her puffy pink marshmallow arms around Boo's neck and burst into tears.

She's exhausted, Tag thought, noticing the fatigue around her eyes again. And then, annoyed that he felt *sympathy* toward her, he told himself it was probably planning the little extravaganza outside that had exhausted her.

Then he noticed Hutch and Boo glaring at him with identical expressions of accusation. He threw up his hands in exasperation and went and found a cell to clean. Hopefully it would keep him busy until the crowd outside had dispersed, Lila had gone home, her uncle had cooled off and his dog had been returned to her senses.

Hopefully it would keep him busy long enough to forget the way he felt when he saw she was still limping.

CHAPTER THREE

"…DONATIONS are pouring in," Lila told her aunt Marla, tossing a raft of envelopes she'd been sorting through into the air. "And the best? A man, Henry, who retired in Spokane, but used to work in maintenance at a big California theme park, thinks he can fix the elves and the reindeer. He's sure he can save the Santa's workshop display!"

When Lila had accompanied Henry to the city storehouse, she'd been dismayed when the town maintenance man hadn't wanted to let her in, and had treated her vaguely as if she was the *enemy.*

When she had finally talked her way past the sentry, her dismay had deepened when she saw what sad shape everyone was in: it wasn't just the mechanics of the animated figurines that was in trouble. The paint had been neglected, and was faded, patchy and peeling. Rather than looking cheery, the elves looked downright spooky.

"Still, I'm trying to put together a work bee for the weekend. Henry's going to bring the special paint—"

She noticed suddenly that despite the good news, her aunt looked distracted. It occurred to her that Marla had not even mentioned the new display of sleds laden with fresh piles of holly and mistletoe at the front door of the store.

Her aunt *always* noticed the new things that came in. She was Miss L. Toe's greatest fan and Lila's biggest supporter.

"Is something the matter?" Lila asked.

Marla sighed. "Oh, Lila, all this is wonderful, but for every piece of mail you've received the Police Department has received one, too. Most of it's addressed to Brody. It's awful. Hate mail."

"He acts as if he couldn't care less, but Paul said he's called in sick twice this week. Brody Taggert has never been sick a day in his life. That poor kid. As if he hasn't had enough to deal with."

First of all, Lila was astonished that anyone would see Brody Taggert as a kid. To her he was one-hundred-percent pure intimidating man. And if she hadn't felt that way before, she certainly had while he *arrested* her.

She'd been so aware of his size, his power, his pure authority. He'd carried himself through that hostile crowd like the alpha male of a wolf pack: confident in his territory, unafraid, indifferent to the challenges of the lesser pack members. She had felt oddly protected, even though she knew the focus of the crowd's hostility had certainly not been on her, but on him.

Not that he deserved it. Her aunt was right. Poor guy. He had just been doing his job.

And that was what he'd looked like on the footage that had aired just a few days ago, first in Spokane, and then, luckily, a slow day for news, around the nation. The human interest aspect of the plight of Santa's Workshop in Snow Mountain had been picked up by media everywhere.

The camera had captured something she had not really been aware of at the time: that the mood in the crowd could have turned on a hair, that the smallest crack in Brody's confidence could have turned that situation very ugly.

But he had handled himself with astounding control. Brody had the look of a man who knew how to get the job done: the look of men who went into battle and gladiator's rings; a chilling calm, a thin veneer over a state of readiness. His expression had been flat and yet there was no mistaking the forbidding look on his features: *Don't mess with me. Don't even think it.*

She'd had that thought again, ridiculous, given the fact she'd been the one he was leading away in cuffs, but there it had been.

The world was a better place because of men like this one.

Lila, looking at herself in those video clips, wished she'd worn her black leather jacket instead of the warmer down-filled parka, and taken a miss on the Santa hat. She had looked tiny beside him, and frightened. The limp had made her look fragile. Still, when she looked at it, she didn't really see Brody *arresting* her. In fact, there was something protective about the way he put his body between her and that moody crowd. She'd felt the same *shiver* again when she reviewed the clips.

Unfortunately, then she had to remember bursting into tears when he'd said, perfectly understandably, too, that he hoped never to see her again.

She tried to tell herself it was the chronic insomnia, the emotion of the day, the disapproval in her uncle's eyes, the fact that the only being in the room who'd sympathized with her was a *dog*.

But in her heart she knew something about Brody Taggert called to her. It called to that place in her that *wanted:* heated looks and stolen kisses, brushes of hands, sizzling awareness.

Brody Taggert awakened the part in her she had deliberately put to sleep, deliberately walked away from: as too dangerous, too unpredictable, too painful, too unlike the world she created in her store, the world that she hoped to create in the town and in her book.

The book which, with all the excitement of the last week, she still had not started, though she was now contemplating beginning with a chapter called *How to Get Your Town to Care About a Perfect Christmas.*

But for now the important thing was that the story of Snow Mountain shutting down their Christmas display had had exactly the effect she intended. It had worked miracles. Three thousand dollars in donations so far!

And Henry. He thought he might be able to have the display ready to light up two weeks before Christmas. She was tentatively setting December 15 as the date they would reopen Santa's Workshop on Snow Mountain.

But this was the first Lila had heard that the Police Department was experiencing an equal and opposite reaction.

And the thought of Brody—she had started calling him that in her mind after Jeanie had called out his full name—getting hate mail made her stomach drop. She was frightened of him, or more accurately of her reaction to him, but to think of him getting hate mail was horrible.

She thought of his eyes: the brown shot through with gold, a glimpse of something she wouldn't quite call gentleness, but something in him that was tender, *hurting,* his mystery.

She could not shake the feeling of *knowing* him. Oh, not what he was showing her, not what he wanted her to believe about him, but who he really was.

"Town Hall's not faring very well, either," Marla said. "Some of the stations have dug up the footage from last year of the burning elf. These are not Snow Mountain's finest moments being aired for the entertainment of America."

That explained the chilly reception at the town storage facility. Lila had the sudden uncertain thought that maybe even if she did manage to get everything fixed, she still had to have the approval of Town Council to put the display back in the park. And she'd managed to alienate them.

Even though she wanted to ask her aunt exactly how mad she'd managed to make everyone, she had to know something else first.

"What do you mean Officer Taggert has had enough to deal with? What do you mean poor *kid?*" Because of the danger of his intrigue, Lila really knew she shouldn't be asking these questions. She considered herself to be a model of self-control, so she was stunned when the questions got asked anyway.

Of course, she reminded herself, the model of self-control had also been sitting on the floor of the police station, sobbing into the fur of a dog.

Insomnia, she excused her weaknesses.

It occurred to her there were parts of herself that she did not know, and that perhaps she could not control.

And when she thought of those *things* in relation to Brody Taggert the shiver inside of her intensified.

It was the wrong time to think of the firm line of his lips, to wonder about their taste, but again, she was aware of losing her hold on control.

If Marla now told her something that made her feel tender toward him and bashed down her wary defenses, she would be in trouble.

But Marla, thankfully, suddenly closed up. She was a

policeman's wife, who kept police business police business, who knew those taciturn kind of men who did that work did not like their personal lives shared, and who obviously knew no one would appreciate sympathy less than Brody Taggert.

"Lila," she said gently, "I really believe you can save Santa's Workshop. But I don't know if it's worth the public relations nightmare that's been created for the Police Department and for the town."

Marla could have said *the public relations nightmare you created for the police department and for the town,* and *for Brody Taggert.*

Lila looked at the distress in her aunt's face and knew, however unwittingly, she had managed to hurt the people who cared about her the most.

After her stalker had dismantled her life with unwanted telephone calls, and gifts and appearances for two years—and then taken her hostage for the six most terrifying hours of her life—who had been there for her? Who had unhesitatingly offered her refuge?

Her uncle Paul and her aunt Marla.

And just like her aunt Marla had protected Brody's personal history right now, she knew her aunt and uncle had done the same for her. There had not been a single whisper since she'd arrived here of what had driven her to this remote corner of the globe, about why she had appeared here so suddenly to open her store.

"What can I do?" she asked her aunt.

Marla smiled tiredly. "I think you've done quite enough, dear."

"No. I made this mess and I can fix it." How? Without tangling more with that man? Without putting herself more firmly in the danger zone, on the collision course with her secret untamable self?

"Some things can't be fixed," Marla said.

"Well," Lila said stubbornly, "most can. Look at the Christmas Display. Doomed. But now there's hope. Isn't there always hope?"

"I don't know," her aunt said. "Don't worry about it, Lila. It will pass. I'm sorry I mentioned it."

Don't do this, her rational side begged. But her wilder side begged, too: live a little dangerously. See what happens next. Put yourself in the path of the oncoming train. You can jump out of the way, just in time, just before disaster hits.

Think it through, her tame side demanded. *If it's a good idea it will still be a good idea tomorrow.*

But her wild side seemed to be all done with listening, with obeying, with being controlled.

Her wild side wanted to see Brody Taggert again, be with him, get to know him, dance with danger.

Not a shred of *that* showed in what she said next.

Oh, no, she did a perfect imitation of little Dorothy Do-Gooder, just trying desperately to right her wrongs.

"Aunt Marla, what if we all worked together to fix the display? The SOS committee, the Town, the Police Department? Wouldn't that make a great follow-up story? How the spirit of Christmas is bringing the whole town of Snow Mountain together? It's like a Christmas miracle. The media will eat it up! We can put Bro—Officer Taggert front and center. He'll be getting fan mail instead of hate mail!"

And I hope it isn't all from me.

Her aunt laughed. "I don't think Brody would go for that. He's the guy who least likes the front and center position."

"He doesn't even have to know the press is going to be there," Lila said stubbornly. "Just tell Uncle Paul to order him to help out."

It wasn't a very nice fact that a man she thought of way more often than she had any right to—a man who was as attractive as any other she had ever seen—would have to be *ordered* to spend time with her.

But he'd made it perfectly—painfully—clear at their last meeting he never wanted to see her again.

She didn't blame him. Not really. But this would be for his own good.

She didn't even want to contemplate the mess she had made last time she had decided that the means justified the end.

"Let me think about it," Marla said uncertainly.

"We have no time to think about it," Lila insisted. "The story will die, and then no one will care. Phone Uncle Paul. Tell him Brody Taggert and as many other police men as he can dig up have to be available Saturday morning at 10:00 a.m."

"Where?" Marla said.

"We need a place big enough to house at least twenty people, maybe more, twelve reindeer, eight elves and Santa Claus. It has to be a place that can handle a little grease and dropped paint."

"Taggert's barn is the only place I can think of that's that big," her aunt said. "That's where we built the Snow Mountain float for the Bloomsday Parade in Spokane."

"Brody Taggert's barn?" she asked.

"He lives on his family's place, just west of town. That's where the barn is."

Brody Taggert's barn. A peek into his personal life,

beyond the uniform. Her wild side was jumping up and down with glee. Her other side was frowning at her with prudish disapproval.

His barn, she told her inner prude, *not his bedroom.*

"If this doesn't go well, we've sent the press right to Brody's front door," her aunt said uncertainly.

"It will go well!" Lila pleaded. "I know it will."

But she wasn't feeling as certain as she made herself sound. Because really, she was sending *herself* to Brody Taggert's front door, and he had said very plainly he never wanted to see her again.

That was wishful thinking in a town this size, but still, she was probably pushing it by setting up shop in his barn.

Well, the barn hadn't been her idea. It wasn't her fault that was where the floats got built. She hadn't asked for a peek at his personal life: it had been handed to her. As if the universe was conspiring with her.

Still she felt a shiver of pure apprehension with toying with something as powerful as chemistry.

After a moment's hesitation, Marla looked at her, smiled ruefully, shook her head and picked up the phone. "Hi, Pete," she said. "Put me through to the chief."

Brody had been watching sourly from his kitchen window for the past few days as the elves arrived one by one at his barn, delivered by volunteers with pickups. And then the reindeer. And finally, before daybreak on Saturday on a big truck, Santa, and guess who was getting out of the truck with Santa, supervising the unloading?

The enemy at the gate.

Not that Lila Grainger was any kind of enemy. Jeez, he'd watched the news, too. She didn't even look like an opponent.

He understood perfectly why he was getting mail. It was a kind of David and Goliath story, him unfortunately being Goliath. Her unfortunately being a rather sexy version of David.

Which was where the *enemy* part came in.

Lila Grainger made him *feel* things, things he had been quite content not to feel for a long time.

The number one thing she made him feel was a longing…for, of all the crazy things, wild strawberries.

And the other thing was this weird desire to *protect* her, though as far as he could tell he was probably the one in need of protection.

He'd do well to remember how the David and Goliath story ended. Things did not go well for Goliath.

He watched her go to the barn, heave unsuccessfully on the doors. He frowned. She was still favoring one foot, he was sure of it.

Well, there was no sense letting her *know* how rattled she made him feel. He'd been in the cop business long enough to know you never let fear show, or uncertainty. Every man had weaknesses. Every man had moments when his courage failed him. But some men had a gift for not letting that show, and he was one of those men.

So, he'd confront her head-on. She would never know how badly he wanted to stay away from her, how badly touching her had made him aware of the hardness of his own world, the imbalance of a world where there was nothing soft.

Even this house, new, was all hard lines, modern and sleek, masculine and without frills. He *liked* it like that: orderly, easy to keep clean, free of knickknacks. Free of sentiment.

He'd succeeded in creating a life without softness, closing away all that tickled at those places in him, as easily as he had closed up the family home that now stood unused on the other side of the barn.

Except Boo, he thought as he shrugged on his jacket. Boo, his one *soft* thing, and now she was going.

A reminder of what *soft* things and tender feelings did to a man: left him vulnerable, stole his strength.

Love was Delilah stealing Sampson's hair.

That pesky word again. *Love.* He shook it from his mind, impatiently, a man shooing away an annoying fly. Boo was already at the back door, the one off the kitchen, humming happily as if she *knew* who had arrived.

His traitor dog usually *warned* him when he was about to get into trouble. Not this time, no sirree, the dog was leading him to the enemy at the gate with a wagging tail and eagerness he had not seen in her in days. Two days in the past week, Boo had been so sick he had not gone to work, not sure she would see the end of the day. Now she seemed improved again, and he was riding the roller coaster of denial and hope.

And that's what love did: made a man helpless when he most wanted to be powerful.

With that thought foremost in his mind, Brody stepped from the darkness of the yard into the light of the barn. Long ago, his father had taken the stalls out, leaving a cavernous space to store and work on farm machinery. That, too, was gone, now, and all that was left was space. Space that was filled right now with elves and reindeer, and one very large Santa.

"Hello," she said, coming out from behind an elf, Boo already attached to her heel. Her hair was caught back in a clasp and she was wearing pink earmuffs and matching mittens, as if it was forty below zero outside. Her nose looked almost as pink as her muffs.

Soft. Not made for this weather, he thought, aware of a certain hopefulness. *She'd quit this town, probably after Christmas, and his life could get back to normal.*

Though at the moment he couldn't think what it was he'd ever liked so much about normal.

That's what she did to him: made his thinking, always so clear, always so practical, now faintly scattered, a whole unexplored area of gray *uncertainty* edging into his nice black-and-white world.

"What a beautiful barn," she said, hugging herself against the chill. "How old is it?"

Was she avoiding looking at him?

He shoved his hands in his own pockets, decided to avoid looking at her, too. "It's been here since my family had the property. A hundred years or so."

"Imagine a family being in one place for a hundred years," she said wistfully. "Someday your children will play in that loft, just the way you did. I can practically hear them laughing."

Then she did look at him, and he at her.

And for a moment it sprang between them: that spark of heat, the life force needing to create, to bring another generation forward, that feeling between a certain man and a certain woman. *This could be it.*

He barely knew her, Brody told himself ferociously. *This couldn't be it, because he simply wasn't allowing it.* He did not think of the past. He did not think of the future. Especially not a future where his children laughed in a hayloft.

He survived by staying grounded in the now. She was not *connected* to him. She had not really heard laughter.

It was no big deal that she knew he had played in the hayloft. That's what kids did. But without warning he heard the ghost of his brother's laughter reverberating off the ancient timbers of the loft. He actually looked up toward that darkened place, then looked quickly away, frowning, *feeling*.

That was what she seemed to be bringing back into his life, whether he was ready for it or not, and he was pretty darn sure he was not. And that was after only a few brief, brief encounters with her.

He shivered.

"Are you cold?" she asked.

"No!" he said, *hating* that she wanted to see things about him that he did not want to show her. The place where he was not tough, not invulnerable, not able to withstand discomfort without flinching.

"I *love* the cold," she announced, just as if he had said *yes*, instead of no. "It feels so clean, so pure, don't you think?"

He had never given one thought to how cold felt. He didn't want to think about how cold felt now. He did not want her fooling with the way he saw his world.

But he bet her kisses would taste like snowflakes. Pure. Clean. Moist. Sweet. He looked at her lips, looked away before she noticed, shoved his hands deeper in his jacket pockets.

As if she hadn't noticed his lack of response, she said, "I can't wait to try skating. And sledding."

See? That was the thing about his thinking. Because he could picture doing those things with her, though he had not skated or sledded for years, and had felt no desire to do either activity. They were parts of his life left behind, that he could not reclaim without being swamped with memories of his brother.

She stuck out her hand rather formally. "Officer Taggert, thanks for the use of your barn."

Like he'd had a choice.

"Call me Brody," he said, but reluctantly, aware he had liked the barrier of his position between them. Liked it very much. Sought refuge in it.

"All right. Brody."

It sounded just as he had known it would, way too personal, like a blessing coming off her tongue. Then he made the mistake of taking her proffered hand.

Something happened. It was as if he had been cold, frozen cold, without somehow knowing it. Not the good kind of cold, either, not the pure, clean kind. And now warmth gnawed at the edges of his world, promising something.

Her hand lingered in his, her eyes met his and held.

They yanked their hands away at the same time.

"I'll make coffee," she stammered.

"I'll—" He looked around, saw a man tinkering with an elf, jerked his thumb at him. "I'll give him a hand."

Neither of them moved. The barn door heaved open and Mrs. Harper and Jamison came in.

Jamison loudly announced, "Cold enough to freeze off a monkey's—"

Jeanie gave Jamison a look.

"—eyelashes," he finished weakly. "Jeanie brought her cookies. I brought chili for lunch. Sounds like the whole fri—uh, darned—town is going to be here."

"You brought chili?" Brody asked, incredulous.

Jamison had brought chili? It was his secret recipe. He only made it for guys' poker night at his place.

"Yeah," Jamison said a little defiantly.

"With or without the secret ingredient?"

"What secret ingredient?" Lila asked innocently.

"Without!" Jamison sputtered.

"Well, that's good," Brody said.

"What's the secret ingredient?" Lila asked again, more insistently.

"Love," Jamison lied slickly.

The dog wasn't the only traitor. The dog wasn't the only one falling under her spell. Only Jamison slid Jeanie Harper a look. It wasn't Lila's spell he was under at all. It was the spell of those cookies.

"Oh, isn't that the sweetest thing?" Lila said.

Only Brody saw the look Jamison shot at him, not sweet at all. *Tell the real secret ingredient and I'll cut out your tongue.* The secret ingredient was supposedly ash from a Cuban cigar.

"Why'd you leave it out?" Jeanie teased him. "The world—or a pot of chili—always needs more love. I bake it into every batch of cookies."

So there they stood, two rough men, two soft women, something humming in the air, softly. Ever so softly.

Thankfully the barn door swung open and another group breezed in on a fresh cloud of cold air.

In fact within an hour, the barn was bustling with activity. As well as the entire SOS Committee, at least thirty people were there, including Marla and Paul. The mayor and most of Town Council came. A half a dozen or so Girl Guides had arrived, and their leader was trying to keep them away from five members of the Icemen, Snow Mountain's Junior B hockey team.

Soon, everybody had found a job: the women sanding and painting, the men gravitating toward where Henry showed them the mysterious workings inside the elves and reindeer. Somebody had brought a portable stereo and Christmas songs were playing. The barn was filled with laughter, joking, chatter.

Brody, after getting a few basics from Henry, had the back off a particularly grumpy looking elf. He didn't do social functions. The last town gathering he'd been at had been his brother's funeral. It seemed since then, when he went somewhere, someone always had to tell him how sorry they were. How much they missed Ethan.

He was aware, *suddenly,* he was missing Ethan.

Naturally he intended to blame Lila, since she had brought up the subject of children laughing in the hayloft.

Still, looking around, Brody was aware of how much Ethan had liked this kind of thing. Community. Service. He'd always been the volunteer counselor at the church summer day camp, the first one with a garbage bag on Highway Beautification Day. Painting a new smile on an elf would have been right up Ethan's alley. Ethan who had been artsy rather than bold, who had been sensitive rather than strong.

They had been opposites all their lives, really, Brody and his brother. It had never been a problem for them, not until Darla.

He shook off the unwanted thoughts, and as he did he became aware that even as he took apart the panels to get at the mechanical workings as Henry had instructed him to do he was more and more aware of *her.*

Of the way she fit in here. Of how wherever she was in the room the laughter followed.

And he was aware of Boo wagging with happiness as she went from person to person greeting them, accepting a pat on the head.

Someone called a coffee break, and Brody took a cup and joined the circle of the people he had lived with his whole life. For the first time in a long time he allowed himself to be a part of it. He told Jeanie Harper he would walk a mile barefoot through a blizzard for her chocolate dipped shortbread.

When he heard one of the hockey players tease Mary Beth Anderson about her new braces, he told her he'd been hearing all over town what a great piece she had played on the piano at the recital. He asked after Mrs. Olive's grandson who was serving with the armed forces overseas. He did not hold himself separate from them.

He had thought it was his job that kept him separate from them. How could you make friends with the guy you would be giving a speeding ticket to next week or next month? How did you chat casually with someone you knew had beaten his wife once?

But now, today, he was aware it was not his job that had kept him separate. It was his sorrow, his fear of connecting, of caring too deeply.

He looked again at the darkness of the loft, felt the warmth of Boo sitting right on top of his feet and surrendered, for the first time since the accident, to the life his brother would have wanted for him. For the first time in a long time he accepted the embrace of his small community, allowed himself to feel the warmth of belonging.

His community gathered around him as though he had never left them, never held himself apart, as if they had just saved his place for when he was ready to come back.

The women teased him, and asked how his folks were enjoying their retirement in Arizona, the men chatted about sports, and the weather and about hunting and fishing. He saw how children had grown and parents had aged. He *felt* his part in it, his history, knew this to be as much his family as his parents in Tucson.

He looked over at Lila. She smiled tentatively, and he could imagine *her* laughter in the hayloft.

A naughty thought. He ordered himself not to smile back, but he must have, because she blushed and looked away as if she was having a few naughty hayloft thoughts of her own.

But just when it felt good to let his guard down, just when he was wondering why he had held on to his aloneness so hard and so long, the barn doors swung open.

The television crew from Spokane had arrived, Jade Flynn breezing through the door, a cameraman, already rolling behind her.

He set down his coffee cup, got up and went out the back door. The cold air felt good. So did being by himself, except for Boo, who had trailed reluctantly out after him.

Boo, who never had a secret agenda, who never did something with a motive, wanting something else in return.

This great community project, this coming together of spirit suddenly felt as commercial as all the rest of it: a manipulation of the media. Not real at all. Just a big show to repair the damage of the last story.

The door squeaked open behind him, and shut again. He didn't turn around, because he didn't have to.

He could smell wild strawberries.

"Did everyone know they were coming except me?" he asked.

"No one ever knows if the media is coming for sure," she hedged. "They have to decide if the story is good."

He turned and gave her a look. "Oh, it's a good story.

Town divided. Town coming back together. What was my part in it going to be?"

"I just thought if you and I could be seen together looking like we were getting along, it might take some of the pressure off you."

"The pressure off me?"

"You know. The hate mail."

He snorted. Lila Grainger, little bit of nothing, was trying to look after *him?* It was insulting. He hated it that anyone, let alone her, would ever think he needed looking after.

"I don't think two letters from a nine-year-old in Connecticut who thinks I'm *nasty* qualifies as hate mail."

"You took two days off work because of it."

He went very still. That was something he didn't want anyone to know about. "Are you spying on me?"

"Of course not. But it's obvious to me you aren't even a teensy bit sick, so why were you off work?"

Something clawed at his throat. He could tell her. He could tell her about Boo. He could have a soft place to fall when it happened.

But there was the little trust thing. Poor cop losing his dog would probably make a great human interest story for the town, bring in even more donations for her stupid Save Our Snow Mountain Committee, bring more people out to her store.

"You know what a great ending to this story would be?" he said quietly. She didn't even recognize the danger in his tone.

"What?" she asked. She didn't even have the sense to back away from him.

"What if I kissed you?" he said. "Wouldn't that make a

nice ending? Arresting you one moment, kissing you the next?"

Her eyes went very wide. Too late, she took a step back from him.

He caught her, pulled her in close, took her lips harshly, angry, punishing. But her softness defeated him.

His clarity was gone.

He could taste wild strawberries and hear children laughing in haylofts. Her lips were like a homecoming to a man who had been at war. Her kiss could make a man forget how damned cruel life could be, her taste could fill him with the most dangerous thing of all: hope. Her lips held this power, even in the face of the fact she had betrayed him. Used his home to forward her cause, to create yet another media circus.

He put her away from him, while he still had the strength, before he believed the whisper of his heart above the stern warning of his head.

"How was that for an ending?" he said, trying to insert a caustic note into his voice when the truth was the sweetness of that kiss was taking the bitterness from him like sugar added to coffee. "Oh, just a sec. Too bad. The cameras missed it." He put enough swear words between them and cameras to do Jamison proud.

He wanted to wipe his lips to make his point, but he saw from the tears gathering like a storm in the blue of her eyes he already had made his point.

And besides, he wasn't quite ready to get rid of the taste of wild strawberries yet.

"And just when I was ready to concede you might be a nice guy," she sputtered angrily, in defiance of the tears that sparkled in her eyes.

"What would make you think that?"

"How nice you were to that little girl with the braces!"

"People can act like a whole lot of things they're not. They can make it look like they want to bring a town together, when all they really want is a story that will bring a whole lot of attention to a town that normally wouldn't get it. A town, that coincidentally, has a brand-new Christmas store in it."

He saw the arrow hit home, was not nearly as satisfied by the direct hit as he thought he would be.

Jade Flynn picked that moment to come out the back door, cameraman trotting behind her, camera on his shoulder. "Here's the two I was looking for. Lila, thanks for the heads-up, what a great story."

Lila sniffed, and scrubbed furiously at her eye. Brody stalked away. Was he going to make her cry every single time he saw her?

Or did she just cry so easily because she was tired? He'd still noticed the circles under her eyes today. It really bugged him that, as angry as he was, he still cared that he'd made her cry.

"I guess," Jade said catching on that the tension was pretty thick out here, "a picture of you two painting a new smile on an elf together is probably out of the question?"

The camera clicked on just in time to catch Brody's smoldering look over his shoulder, and then a careless salute, middle finger up.

Ignoring the activity in his barn, the overflowing of cheer and goodwill, Brody retreated to his house and his TV set. Boo threw up under the coffee table, and he told himself it was because people had been unable to resist her big brown eyes begging for cookies. It wasn't because her illness was progressing. It wasn't. But his explanation to himself held the hollow ring of a lie, of a man in denial.

Brody Taggert needed, almost desperately, to believe that kiss, delivered with such fierce anger, had ended whatever had been simmering between Lila and him.

But again he felt the hollow ring of a lie, of denial. In truth that kiss had opened another door, added another dimension to a relationship that was already way too complicated.

He wanted to feel *satisfied* that he had driven home his point that he was not going to have his life manipulated so that Lila Grainger could create her perfect story. He had definitely driven home that point. She'd been crying, hadn't she?

The problem was that he didn't feel satisfied.

Not at all.

He felt guilty. Of all the stupid reasons for a man to kiss a woman, anger would rate number one on his list.

And even worse than feeling guilty and stupid, he felt hungry. For another taste of those lips.

Brody Taggert realized, suddenly and uneasily, what had just happened to him. He had reacted to Lila Grainger with pure, unfettered emotion.

How was he ever going to face the shattering emptiness of another Christmas alone if his emotions got out of control? How was he going to face the stark loneliness of a life where his days did not begin with his dog licking his face in the morning in joyous greeting if he allowed himself to be emotionally weak?

He knew the solution: Lila was triggering emotional reactions. No more Lila. But somehow that resolution, instead of bringing him the comfort of a man firmly back in control, made him feel emptier than ever.

CHAPTER FOUR

SHE had such good intentions, Lila thought forlornly. After a week of hard work the fully repaired and painted elves were being brought in to Bandstand Park. The reindeer would arrive tomorrow, followed by Santa. She had not personally hazarded another visit out to Brody Taggert's barn, though.

That kiss had been a little too revealing. He had, she knew, intended for it to be punishing. Instead she had felt his stark loneliness so acutely it had brought tears to her eyes. Instead she had felt her own vulnerability to him so sharply it had felt like stepping on glass all over again.

So, she had busied herself here with other volunteers, rigging the park with enough new Christmas lights—LED, the energy efficient kind—that Snow Mountain would be seen winking and blinking merrily from space, with an energy bill that would have thrilled Scrooge.

On December 15, as dusk was falling, in a grand ceremony, everything would be plugged in and lit up. The high school band would play, the Baptist ladies' church choir would sing holding candles. Hot chocolate would be served. All the downtown businesses were staying open late. It was Snow Mountain just as she had wished it could be. Well, there was no snow yet, but the locals informed her it was too early for snow.

Why did she feel so hollow? As if she didn't care about the park anymore or lights that could be seen from space, or whether the choir had white candles or red ones?

It was because the book was still stalled, she tried to convince herself. She had thought maybe she could begin with a chapter on energy efficient Christmas lights, but it had turned out she couldn't think of that much to say about them.

She was lying to herself anyway. She wasn't feeling apathetic about bringing Christmas back to Snow Mountain because her book was stalled.

It was because of that kiss.

One little kiss, and she was ready to write off her whole life as an unmitigated disaster. Well, not just because of the kiss. First there had been her foot, then the arrest and then the kiss.

Something in her stomach dropped every single time she thought of the heat of his lips on hers, the fire in his eyes that had not been completely about anger, the answering fire in her belly that had not been about anger at all.

Thankfully Jade Flynn had taken pity on Snow Mountain, and had decided Brody's one finger salute was inappropriate, because the edited segment had showed Lila and her uncle and the mayor painting the new smile on the elf, and Brody's name and image had not been mentioned or shown.

To anyone looking closely enough, Lila's eyes might have seemed puffy, and her makeup a little smeared, but she was sure everyone thought she had cried tears of joy for the saving of Christmas in Snow Mountain.

Her eyes were always faintly puffy from lack of sleep anyway.

Brody had kissed her in fury. She knew that.

So it didn't say much for her that the memory of that kiss haunted those long hours in the night when she couldn't sleep anyway, made her torment herself with forbidden thoughts and dream impossible dreams.

Of smoldering eyes, and the magnificent beauty of the muscled male body. And gentler dreams, too, of little children laughing in haylofts.

"I think," her aunt Marla said, standing back, a string of LED lights over her shoulder, "it's missing a Christmas tree. Wouldn't that look nice? A twenty-foot blue spruce, decorated in all blue lights?"

"It's good enough," Lila said, desolately. "It's too late to get a tree."

Her aunt looked askance at her. "That kind of tree grows thick as hair on a dog's back in these parts. We'll just go pick one out and cut it down. I'm sure your uncle Paul will do it."

"Maybe I could go with him," Lila said, trying to at least act as if she had some enthusiasm, trying to at least pretend she was the person she had been three weeks ago. "I'd love to actually see a Christmas tree harvested."

And wouldn't that make a great place to start the book? Going out and getting the tree, the old-fashioned way, too. Not from the Christmas tree lot, not from the fake tree department of the local big-box store.

"Great. I'll get Paul to pick you up at around eleven next Saturday. Maybe pack a bit of a lunch. Just in case he's grouchy about it."

"If he's going to be grouchy about it, never mind." She said it reluctantly, because going to get a tree really could kickstart the book, and maybe it could occupy her enough that she would escape her preoccupation with Brody for a few hours. But on the other hand Lila felt like she had learned her lesson about asking people to do things for the greater good when they really didn't want to do them.

"Just pack a few of Jeanie Harper's shortbread cookies. The chocolate-dipped ones."

Brody liked those ones best, too. That little yearning, naked and helpless, leaped up in her.

"Chocolate-dipped shortbread," Lila said with false heartiness.

She turned away before she caught the fact her aunt was looking at her with far more knowing than she would have liked.

Brody pulled up in front of Lila Grainger's door. Nice part of town. Mature trees, big yards, old, well-kept houses. Hers, not surprisingly, looked like it could be the cottage from Snow White—a tiny house sat under a steeply pitched mossy roof. Deep windows were diamond paned and carved shutters bracketed them on the outside.

Brody resisted the temptation to honk the horn of the truck, which would be a betrayal of the irritation he felt that their paths were being forced to cross again.

"Go get a Christmas tree for the park with her," Hutch had ordered him. "And wipe that look off your face. Be cheerful about it, for God's sake."

Jamison had snickered in the background.

The chief had shot Jamison a look. "I wouldn't be so smug if I were you, Santa."

But Brody was lost in his own thoughts. *Be cheerful about spending more time with Lila Grainger, and her lips, and his own tenuous hold on his emotions around her?*

"I don't want to do it," Brody had said.

The answer was predictable. "Tough."

"Is there going to be a bunch of cameras there when I get back with the tree?" Brody asked, realizing he'd capitulated without too much of a fight considering what he had at stake.

"You just aren't that big a deal, boy," his boss had told him shortly. "The truth is Marla told me to go get a tree. A big one. I haven't handled a chain saw in over ten years. I'd probably limb myself instead of the damned tree."

That, unfortunately, was probably the truth, so Brody told himself he was doing it to save his boss's limbs as much as because he'd been told to. But be cheerful about it? *Sheesh.* He hadn't had one single thing to be cheerful about since he'd arrested Lila Grainger.

He was still getting hate mail, especially from one very persistent little kid in Connecticut who must have either missed the follow-up story, or been able to discern from Lila's distressed face that all was still not as it appeared to be in Snow Mountain.

Just as he'd predicted the pre-Christmas fallout was starting all over town. Last night, Tag had waited outside the bar to keep Mike Stevens from getting in his car and driving. Mike was generally a good guy: Tag had played hockey with him for years. Mike was strong, reliable and steadfast.

Mike and his wife were three weeks from having a baby. Everyone knew Mike had been laid off work at the mill and the financial pressure to provide for his new family was killing him.

"Do you know what a bassinet's worth?" he'd slurred drunkenly when Tag had driven him home last night. "That's what she wants for Christmas. A bassinet for the baby. I don't even know how I'm going to come up with rent."

Then, the Murphy girl, fifteen going on twenty, the one with trouble written all over her, had been caught shoplifting and he'd been sent to pick her up from the store.

In the back of the cruiser, her tough girl facade had broken. A video game for her little brother for Christmas. *Tower of the Rebels. Fifty bucks,* she'd said bitterly through her tears. *He might as well have wished for a ticket to the moon.*

And Brody's dog was fading by the day. This was the first time he'd brought her along with him for nearly two weeks.

And as if his life wasn't bad enough, he couldn't get the taste of Lila Grainger's lips or the look of her eyes out of his mind. Now he had to get a tree with her. Which he hoped he could do in about twenty minutes. Which was probably going to be the longest twenty minutes in his life now that he'd been fool enough to *taste* her.

Be cheerful?

How could he be cheerful when he could not be at all certain he was only here because he'd been ordered. Not at all.

Maybe he was here because the taste of her lips and the scent of wild strawberries drew him back, irresistibly, illogically, insanely.

Boo barely opened an eye when he got out of the truck.

"Stay here," he said unnecessarily, since the dog had not moved. "I'll be right back."

He rang the doorbell, and she came and answered. He stood looking at her, feeling awkward and tense, as if he was picking her up for a first date.

Not, he told himself sternly.

"Oh," she said, stopping dead in her tracks. "You."

"You were expecting?"

"My uncle."

"He couldn't make it." Cop loyalty prevented him from saying Paul was scared of cutting off his own limbs, because he was sure Paul didn't want his niece to know he was scared of anything.

"I'll go a different day. When he can make it."

"It'll only take twenty minutes. Half an hour. Let's get it over with."

He meant that in every possible way, as if by spending part of an hour with her, he could flush that kiss from his system, erase it with all the new ways she could be annoying.

For instance, right now, she had one earring in, the other dangled from her hand.

He could tell her earrings were not necessary for an excursion into the woods to chop down a tree, but then it would be way too apparent he had noticed, and then he couldn't be *annoyed* by it.

While he was noticing, her ears were dainty, and for a strange moment he had the forbidden thought of nipping one with his teeth.

And maybe that was the real truth of it: this thing between he and Lila Grainger would be over with when it had followed its path to its natural conclusion.

And he had a feeling that wasn't going to be getting a Christmas tree.

He took a step back, one foot resting on the top stair, now. "Maybe you're right. Your uncle. A different day."

"No," she said looking at him with regal dislike. "Maybe *you're* right. Let's get it over with."

"Okay," he said.

"Okay," she said.

Don't look at her lips, he ordered himself. *Or her ears.*

"You'll have to come in. Just for a sec. I'm not quite ready."

Before he could tell her he would rather wait in the truck, she had turned away, and he didn't want her to think he was *scared* to come in.

So that's how he found himself standing in the landing of her house, right inside the front door. He frowned as he watched her disappear. Was she still limping?

From where he stood he could see a real stone fireplace in the living room, already hung with socks. Out of range of his vision, he could tell she had her Christmas tree up because he could smell the pine.

He regarded her room with a policeman's eye. The way people lived could tell you an awful lot about them.

Not that he needed to know a single thing more about Lila Grainger. Her lips had pretty much said it all.

But her living room should have reassured him. No matter what that kiss had said about how compatible they might be in certain arenas, it was more than obvious to him they were exact opposites.

A plump yellow sofa and a large ottoman took up most of the room. There were bookcases, and a single teacup on a side table. He craned his neck to see where the television was, and could plainly see there wasn't one.

It was the room of someone who liked solitary reading better than entertaining, he thought, and had to firmly stop himself from attaching a positive judgment to that.

Who cared if she threw a party every night?

He did, and he didn't like it one little bit that he did.

Somehow, in the small amount of time Lila had been in Snow Mountain she had managed to make her space colorful and warm, *homey,* a reflection of who she was.

Not a girl you stole kisses from, not even in anger.

Especially not in anger. Not a girl where you let things follow through to their natural conclusion.

She was the kind of girl who was wholesome, and decent, optimistic about life, probably a positive thinker.

A guy like him could probably wreck all those qualities pretty darn quick.

She was the kind of girl who was traditional: her house told him that. She would stand at the front of a church one day, dressed in white. She would never live with a man before exchanging vows with him. When she had kids, she would read them stories, and bake them cookies, volunteer at the school, teach them right from wrong.

She probably wouldn't even let them watch television!

There was nothing wrong with that. Nothing at all. He was glad Paul's niece was like that.

He just knew he himself could not be trusted with such wholesomeness, such sugarcoated dreams. He was too broken, too torn up inside, too much of a realist.

Lila Grainger needed someone nice like the preacher's son, who was working on his doctorate in Seattle.

Brody thought he'd put a bug in Paul's ear about that. Much relieved that he had managed, on the basis of her decor, to separate his life from hers, he looked around once more.

He had not lived in a place that felt *homey* since he had left home. A television went a long way in making a man feel at home. The bigger it was, the more at home he felt.

Still, Brody Taggert could have sworn he hadn't missed those homey little touches—paint and prints, throw rugs and knickknacks. But at this very moment, he was aware he had.

The memory came, as they all did, without any kind of warning.

Ethan, at eighteen. They'd been wrestling, Ethan having

something to prove all the time since developing a crush on Brody's girlfriend, Darla. Now they were standing there with Mom's broken cranberry glass wine decanter at their feet, wondering what the hell to do now.

Funny, he couldn't remember what they'd done, only the broken glass, the look of distress on his brother's face. Without warning, he felt lonely, and turned from the warmth of that cozy living room to look out at his truck, to see if the dog had her face pressed to the window, waiting for him.

She did, something so normal, he felt relieved.

But then he noticed Lila's front door.

And the locks on it. Lots and lots of locks. Most people in Snow Mountain couldn't be convinced to use the one lock they had on the handle of their door. He bent closer to inspect.

Four in all. Dead bolts. So brand-new that the metal was shiny. Plus, one of those chain things, and a newly drilled security peephole.

His first impression of her had been correct, that night he had startled her at her store. She was scared of something. Really scared.

What Brody Taggert wanted more than anything else was to move Lila Grainger right up to the number one position on his People I Find Annoying list. Or to make her the preacher's son's problem. But those locks made him *feel* something else.

Protective. Faintly angry at some unknown opponent.

She came back into the living room. Definitely still limping.

"I'm trying to figure out what to wear to go get a tree," she said. "I've never done anything like this before."

Which forced him to look at her way more closely than he wanted to because he was going to be responsible for her safety up there on the mountain, and she was from Florida, where they didn't know the first thing about dressing for even moderately cold weather.

She was dressed in snug jeans and a cable knit sweater, a fur-trimmed dark brown vest on top of that.

She held up a pair of bright pink-and-white-striped mittens for his approval.

First the *homey* house and now this: poster girl for a hot chocolate ad: wholesome, beautiful.

Girl least likely to be arrested. Most likely to be happy with the preacher's son. Least likely to have her front door locked up like Fort Knox.

"Yeah, that'll do," he said out loud. To himself he repeated the mission, *Let's get this over with.*

She suddenly was scrutinizing what he was wearing.

Jeans, T-shirt, sheepskin-lined jean jacket. He wasn't sure why he wished for his uniform. Something to hide behind, something to cut that awareness that suddenly tingled in the air between them.

Don't look at her lips, he ordered himself again. But he did.

"That doesn't look very warm," she said.

Don't look at her ears, he ordered himself, but he did that, too.

"It's thirty degrees Fahrenheit out there. Practically balmy for this part of the world," he pointed out as she slipped a toque, the same color as her mitts, over her ears. Even though he'd ordered himself not to look at them, he was disappointed when they were covered up.

"There's supposed to be a storm coming. If it's below

freezing that could mean snow at last!" She tried not to sound hopeful and failed. "You should dress warmer."

"I've been taking care of myself for a long time," he said flatly. "I don't need anyone to do it for me."

It was a warning and they both knew it.

She blushed, turned to her boots, which looked like they were Arctic rated to minus forty, with huge pom-pom things that looked like they had killed a few rabbits to make them.

Ridiculous things. Adorable.

"How's your foot?" he asked when she winced putting them on.

"My foot? Oh, *that*. Fine."

"You're still limping."

"I know. What an awful place to get a cut. It takes forever to heal."

Okay, he ordered himself, *leave it.* "Are you checking it? Making sure it's not infected?"

He regretted the show of concern immediately, because she folded her arms across her chest and looked at him with warning. A reminder that this was the woman—looking so innocent in her pink mittens—who was responsible for the fact he'd gotten a series of snotty letters from a little girl in grade five who wanted to let him know she thought he was *mean*. And also *nasty*.

This was the woman who was responsible for the fact the chief seemed to think Tag should now single-handedly rescue the image of the Snow Mountain Police Department, even though when he'd arrested her, he'd only been following orders.

"It's fine," she said. "My foot is fine. I've been looking after myself for a long time, too, Brody Taggert."

He liked her ears and her lips and her eyes, and the way his name sounded coming off her lips.

He wondered if that meant he was doomed.

More likely she would be the *doomed* one if she ever ended up with someone as cynical about life—and Christmas—as him. Not that he was ever going to let that be a choice. That they would end up together. Not ever.

He let himself out the door, watched with interest as she came behind him, carrying what looked to be a picnic basket. She set it down to lock the door, and his eyes slid over to it. A thermos. Sandwiches. Cookies. A damned outing.

His attention went back to the door. He watched with interest as she carefully locked two of the dead bolts.

She looked up, caught him looking, looked quickly away. "I figure anyone trying to get in would probably unlock two and lock the other two." He must have let his skepticism show because she said, firmly, "That's how criminals think."

"You don't even have a TV," he said. "Criminals like TVs." So did he, which sealed the fact they could never be together, him and her, not ever. Just too different. Thank God.

"I have a TV, I just keep it in a cabinet."

A TV that was hidden was almost as bad as not having one at all.

Now he was feeling a touch querulous. "And don't think your brush with the law made you any kind of expert on the criminal mind. They'd take one look at all those locks and smash in your basement window."

She became very pale.

"Sorry," he said, thinking she hadn't enjoyed his attempt at humor about her recent arrest. *So much for cheery, Chief.*

But she hadn't even noticed that. She was staring at her basement window with consternation.

"Isn't it awfully small?" she asked.

"You'd be surprised what people can squeeze through."

"Oh," she said in a small voice, standing frozen to the spot, staring at the window.

"Have you got something in there you're worried about?" Any TV that could be successfully *hidden* could not possibly be big enough to worry about.

She shook her head. "I guess I can get bars for it."

"What are you so afraid of?" he asked, that protective thing humming deep inside him, like a drumbeat calling a warrior to the fight. One of those *emotional* responses that he was so determined to be wary of.

She lifted her chin, the very same look she had given him when he'd arrested her.

"I'm not afraid of anything," she said.

But he knew now, just as he had known then, that it was a lie. He shrugged. So she didn't want to tell him. So what? He didn't really want to exchange confidences with her, either.

He held open the passenger side door for her, he had to shove Boo into the middle seat. Boo was thrilled at her arrival, the first show of enthusiasm he had seen from the dog in days.

And when Boo placed her big head on Lila's lap and began to drool happily, Lila didn't even say it was gross. He forgave her a little bit for the hate mail he was getting, for her lack of a television. But not for the fact she was making him *feel* again, when it felt so much safer not to.

"This was nice of you," she said finally, after the silence between them became oppressive. She must have decided it was time to change the tone of the day. "You must have volunteered to come on your day off."

Volunteered. Military style. You, you and you.

"I'm not a nice person," he said, setting up the defenses against future kisses. "You might as well not even think it."

"Ha," she said. "Tell it to someone who didn't see you save the day for a little girl who was self-conscious about her new braces."

"You're reading too much into that."

"How about lending your barn for a cause you don't even believe in?"

He didn't admit that he found himself being kind of glad the park would be back to normal soon. And hopefully his life.

But the dog sighing on the seat beside him reminded him there really was no normal. What was normal for him now would not be his normal by next year. Maybe even not by next week.

"Here's something that should renew your faith in humanity," she said, snapping her fingers, as if she'd totally forgotten the mission was to get this over with, not to restore his faith in humanity, "I've had five thousand dollars worth of donations come in."

He groaned. He flipped on the windshield wipers against the first flakes of snow. "I don't want to know about it."

"Why?"

"Are you a licensed charity?"

"Oh, for heaven's sake," she said, and then caught the grim cast of his face. "Are you always so cheerful?"

"Yes." He looked straight ahead, but the cab of his truck seemed to be getting smaller by the minute. The scent of wild strawberries was growing strong in here. He opened the window a hair.

"For the dog," he said, when she looked askance. She

pulled her scarf tighter around her neck, as if she was about to face a blizzard and forty below.

"Did you grow up here?" She was determined to get a conversation going.

"Yes." He offered nothing else. He didn't want to do this. Small talk. He was terrible at it, something he'd never regretted.

"What was it like growing up here?" she asked wistfully, looking out the window of the truck. "It's so beautiful. Look, snow!"

They were off the main highway now, moving up Snow Mountain on an old forestry road. At each clearing they reached, through a veil of faster and faster falling snow, they would see the valley stretched below them, like a postcard, fields, old barns and in the distance, the town.

Sudden pictures of him and his brother, always outdoors, hunting, fishing, climbing, hiking came into his mind. He longed for what his normal had once been.

"It was okay," he said, deliberately wanting to shut her out.

But she was not going to be shut out. "What was your favorite thing about growing up here?"

He could have said anything. He could have said hunting or fishing or swimming or climbing trees.

But he didn't. He said. "Picking wild strawberries." He didn't know why he said that, probably because of the scent in the truck.

"Strawberries grow wild here?"

He nodded. "A few. They're very small. You can spend a whole day looking for them and maybe get a cup. My mom used to love wild strawberries more than anything. If you offered her a glass of champagne or a handful of strawberries, she'd pick the strawberries."

Suddenly he remembered how they'd made up for busting the cranberry glass. On his last day with his brother.

"Your parents still live here?"

"No, they retired in Arizona." That wasn't the whole truth. The whole truth was when people got attached to what they thought *normal* was, when it changed they couldn't handle it.

His mother had never been the same after Ethan. Nothing had ever been the same. Not their house, not this town, not Christmas or Thanksgiving, or birthdays or the Fourth of July or the opening day of hunting season. Nothing had ever been the same.

Especially not his heart.

Because once upon a time, a long time ago, when he believed in normal and innocence, wouldn't his heart have been open to a girl exactly like this one?

"Do you have any family here?"

"No."

"Will you go spend Christmas with your parents, then?"

"I pulled duty."

"Didn't you work on Thanksgiving, too?"

"Yeah," he said, but he contemplated that she *knew.* Had she asked or had it just come up in conversation? She would have had dinner with Paul and Marla.

He *always* pulled holiday duty. He considered that to be just about the only perk of being the new guy on the job. After their first Christmas without Ethan, his father had taken him aside and said, "It's just too hard on your mother, trying to make everything normal. Next year, let's just get together after the holidays." And it had been like that ever since.

"Oh, that's too bad."

"Terrible," he said, and for some reason he thought of

the faraway look in his mom's eyes at this time of year, and his voice roughened with the memory.

He could feel Lila's eyes on him, full of questions. Like did he have brothers and sisters, and did he go to church on Sunday and did he drink beer, and all those *normal* little details two people getting to know each other wanted to find out.

Except that he did not want her to get to know him. And he did not want to get to know her.

He had been doing just fine with his heart in armor, and he planned to keep it that way.

So he slammed on the brakes so hard the dog had to scramble to stay on the seat.

"There's some good trees," he said.

Despite his optimism about the twenty-minute tree trip, it was more like an hour before she picked the tree she wanted: a huge blue spruce, twenty-feet high that was going to be a nightmare to get down and to load into his truck.

But a challenge was just what he needed right now.

He could feel her eyes on him as he started the chain saw, did the undercut, moved to the other side of the tree.

The tree fell without drama, slowly, and he cut the bottom of the trunk, then bucked the tree—cleared the lower branches—for her.

"I brought a snack. Hot chocolate. Some sandwiches." As if she sensed him weakening, "Jeanie Harper's cookies, chocolate dipped. You look like you need a break."

Her eyes were on him with *what?*

Interest. There it was. That dangerous little sizzle again. Time to winch the tree into the back of the truck and get out of here. The snow was falling in huge, heavy flakes now.

Lila tilted her head back, caught one on her tongue,

closed her eyes as if she was tasting heaven. Her enjoyment of that simple pleasure made it seem less urgent to leave.

Then Boo appeared from the trees, a pinecone in her mouth. She dropped it at Lila's feet and barked.

"What's she want?" Lila asked, laughing, when the dog barked again.

"She wants you to throw the pinecone for her," he said. He had not seen Boo play with a pinecone for a long time, and suddenly he was very aware his *normal* was going to be changing again very soon.

How many moments left like this? With his dog wagging her tail, chasing after a pinecone? He had to take these moments that were given to him.

Suddenly the moment seemed so beautiful it hurt his eyes. A young woman in a sweater and a vest and pink mittens throwing the pinecone for a dog who thought she was young again.

When Lila brought out the picnic basket and spread a plaid blanket on the thickening cover of snow, he didn't complain. He had lived here all his life and never, not even once, had a picnic in the snow.

Perhaps this, too, was a moment he was being given. One that, if he turned his back on, he might regret later.

So, he gathered branches and built a fire and then he sat, and took his dog's head in his lap and scratched her ears, and drank cocoa and ate ham sandwiches and chocolate-dipped shortbread cookies without letting one single thought about what the future held intrude on that moment.

Besides, there was simply no telling when or if he was ever going to get Jeanie's cookies again.

"This is so much fun," she said. "Do you know I've never done anything like this before?"

"Picnics in the snow not a big pastime in Florida?" he said.

She stuck out her tongue at him. "I meant getting the tree. Christmas trees are hard to come by in Florida. Real ones. My mom had an artificial tree that she left completely decorated in the garage. I hated that tree."

Don't ask, he told himself. "Is that why you came here? Real trees?"

"Don't laugh, but that's part of it. I remember coming here for Christmas once when I was ten. Everybody had a real tree. And there was real snow. That's what I remembered most about it. Everything seemed *real.*"

"I don't know why you're so anxious to bring the elves back then. They aren't real. As phony as it comes, actually."

She smiled. "Well, when I was ten they seemed real. I *loved* them."

"You're in a funny business for a lady who claims to like reality," he said. "You're kind of peddling fantasy, aren't you?"

She looked hurt. "I prefer to think of it as magic. Don't you think some things are magical and unexplained? Don't you think Christmas is one of those things? A time of miracles?"

He was silent, and then he said, "I had to arrest a little girl who was shoplifting a gift for her brother that was hopelessly out of the family's price range. A video game. *The Tower of the Rebels.* You know what? She didn't take one single thing for herself. I've arrested lots of teenage girls who are lifting lipstick or perfume, stuff for *themselves.* This was different. It makes it kind of hard for me to get the *magic.* Sorry."

Even as he said it, though, he was aware the sharing had not done what he intended. He had intended for her to get a glimpse of the real *real* world. But instead, he felt by telling her, a burden he carried, without even knowing how much it bothered him, was lifted a bit, not such a weight in his own heart.

"Oh, Brody," she said, "Oh, Brody."

He saw he had lightened his own load by giving it to her. He was annoyed with himself for telling her. Even more annoyed how he *felt*.

He hadn't had so many pesky feelings nipping at him like a small dog harassing a ball, since…

Since his brother had died.

That part of him had shut down. Thankfully. He didn't want it brought back to life, so he deliberately misunderstood her.

"I know. I'm an awful person, and I'm getting the mail every day to prove it."

"I never said you were awful. I meant it was awful about the little girl."

"See, that's the thing, Lila. While you're peddling the fantasy, elves in parks and purple Christmas trees in store windows, there's a reality out there that you wouldn't like one little bit. Even in Snow Mountain."

"That tree in my store window is not purple!" she said, evading the issue or deliberately not getting it. "It's lavender."

"Who cares?" he snapped.

The moment was gone, the sympathetic light doused in her eyes and so he kicked snow on the fire and doused that, too. The picnic was spoiled.

"The weather is turning," he said. "I better get that tree in the truck and get us down off this mountain."

Still, as he struggled with the tree, the dog pleaded with her to toss pinecones again. For a few brief moments, watching her taste snow on the tip of her tongue and toss pinecones for his dog, sitting sipping hot chocolate in the smoke of a fire, something in him had *hoped*.

For what, he wasn't quite sure. A life with laughter in it? Someone to share his burdens with? A life of simple pleasures: going out on a snowy day to get the tree, campfires, a good dog sniffing a picnic blanket for crumbs of the world's best cookies?

Things were always just a little more complicated than that. They were as *different* as two people could be, a fact that could be disguised by strawberry kisses, but only temporarily.

"Christmas is saved in Snow Mountain!" she said, when he'd finally loaded the tree, as if she was still annoyingly determined to *fix* his mood.

But he was aware Boo was slumped at her feet now, spent in a way a little pinecone chasing would not have spent a healthy dog.

"No, it's not," he said grimly. "Lila Grainger's fantasy is saved. The little kid who swiped a toy for her brother has the same day waiting for her as always."

My dog is still going to die, even though for a moment, watching her chase pinecones, maybe I really did want to believe in a time of miracles.

Hope could be a terrible thing in a hard world.

"You know what?" Lila said, "A person who spent too much time around you would probably catch grumpy from you like a bad virus."

Bingo, he thought. Out loud he said, "Get in the truck."

CHAPTER FIVE

LILA was not sure how things had turned so sour. One minute she'd been having a moment out of a Christmas dream: handsome man, hot chocolate, snowflakes, even a dog to complete the picture of holiday cheer. Every detail was perfect: even the air was laden with the sharp scent of the freshly fallen tree and the smoke from the fire.

For one suspended moment in time she had been allowed to enjoy perfection, a moment worthy of a Christmas card. She had even thought, relieved beyond belief, that she had been correct that this would be the perfect way to start her book. Of course having a perfect Christmas would begin with Chapter One: Getting the Perfect Tree.

But then she had looked at his lips, remembered their taste, the sizzling intensity of them taking her own lips, and the sudden dip of her stomach hadn't matched her wholesome holiday picture at all.

And then, Brody's mood had shifted as restlessly as the wind, which had also suddenly shifted, blowing smoke in her face. It had eased sneakily into her mind that despite how nice snow made everything *look* it was darned cold. Even with the blanket, her butt was starting to feel uncomfortably cold, tingly, then numb.

Plus, how could this be the starting point for her book: a book about innocence and wonder, tradition and family, when she was being totally captivated by thoughts that might be considered, well, *wanton*.

There was no way a woman could watch Brody Taggert fell a tree and be thinking strictly innocent thoughts afterward. Or even be admiring the tree, for that matter. Or even thinking about the tree for that matter, no matter how perfect it might be.

Brody felling the tree: a symphony of male strength, so sure of himself, so comfortable with his own power, so competent in his world.

Watching him cut down the Christmas tree had made her so aware of him. And then the moments on the blanket, him stretched out comfortably, lying on his back, staring up at the sky, letting the snowflakes gather in the thick tangle of his lashes, the dog draped across him with utter contentment.

And her preoccupied, not with pressing thoughts of her book or the fact fetching a tree might be an ideal starting point, but with wondering if they were going to kiss each other again. Not in anger this time, either.

Except, suddenly, without warning, his mood had shifted, he had kicked snow on the fire, and they were on their way back down the mountain.

Maybe starting with getting the tree was a bad idea, anyway.

"Do you think cutting down a live Christmas tree is controversial?" she asked him. Talking about anything would be better than the grim silence that filled the truck.

"Controversial?" He looked amazed and then annoyed.

"You know, not an environmentally sound idea."

"Cloning human beings is *controversial*."

"Artificial trees are probably better for the environment." Somehow starting her book with a chapter on selecting the perfect artificial tree was not as appealing, particularly in light of the ghastly white plastic needle one she had shared her childhood with.

"I guess how good an artificial tree is for the environment would depend on how it was made, wouldn't it? How many toxic substances the tree factory melted down and then pumped into the air afterward? And how people dispose of them when blue ones become more popular than green ones, or pink ones or white ones?"

The thing about a man like that was he would make you look at the world differently. He would challenge all your beliefs. You would be trying to write a book about creating the perfect Christmas, and thinking of a little girl stealing a gift for her brother.

A man like him could wreck a plan for a perfect life without half trying.

She shot him a look. He was squinting out through the thickening snow; she noticed he had both hands on the steering wheel.

She realized he *wanted* the animosity. He wanted distance between them. Which meant he had been feeling something, too.

She sighed. Her complicated way of thinking was probably why she was having so much trouble starting her book. It was really black-and-white: if he wanted distance between them, that was a warning sign.

A warning sign that she could get hurt, particularly if she didn't want distance between them.

Which, of course, she did!

They came to a steep incline, he geared down, the back end of the truck slid sideways.

She gasped, the feeling so unexpected, so out-of-control, and he glanced at her, looked right back to the road.

"Just a little slippery," he said, the edge gone from his voice, trying to calm her. "Nothing to worry about."

But why would he even mention there was nothing to worry about if there truly wasn't? If there was really nothing to worry about he might have said, "So what are you doing tonight for supper?" or "Doesn't Jeanie Harper make the best shortbread cookies ever?"

She watched him, his hands, the road, came to the conclusion that the driving was *challenging,* but nothing he hadn't handled a zillion times before.

"Is it going to be like this all winter?" she asked him. "I'll be scared to drive."

"Your uncle can give you a few winter driving lessons," he said. Her uncle, not him, reminding her just how unlikely it was that he would have ever said, "What are you doing for supper tonight?" or at least not in the context of what he was *also* doing for supper.

She took a deep breath, recognizing her mind was babbling to itself, nervous. She gasped again when the truck slid. Her heart felt like it was going to pound out of her chest.

Once, she had enjoyed new experiences. "Sorry," she muttered when he looked askance at her, "I was involved in an *incident* last year. I have a bad startle reflex now."

If he asked her what it was, she had the horrible feeling she would tell him, unburden herself right here and right now, as if he didn't have enough to think about just getting them safely off the mountain.

"Yeah," he said. "I kind of figured maybe you'd had something happen."

"Did my uncle say something?" she asked, aghast.

"No, ma'am, all the locks on your door did."

A man who missed nothing. But it was the lack of judgment in his firm voice, the unexpected compassion, that made her feel suddenly safe with him. As if she could trust him.

She looked at him, really looked. His face was calm, his hands light on the steering wheel. He even reached out and fiddled with the radio at one point.

But the reception mirrored the storm, static-distorted and thick.

Lila felt glad he was obviously so familiar with this area, because she could now barely make out the road against a sea of white. The tracks where the truck had come up the hill were completely erased by the snow. The world was turning white around them with astounding speed.

She began to feel quite safe: Brody so focused on the road, the dog unworried, fast asleep on her lap, the heat pumping out of the heater enveloping her in warmth. Even her butt was beginning to thaw out.

She should have known by now: it was always when she let her guard down that she got blindsided.

The deer jumped out from her side, a dark, swift shadow materializing just off the front bumper.

One minute there was nothing, and then he was there, a beautiful antlered male, monstrously large, blacking out the storm as he filled the view in front of them.

"Deer!" she cried out an unnecessary warning.

"Elk," he corrected her mildly.

She didn't see anyway they could avoid a collision, but

Brody slammed the truck into a lower gear, heaved on the steering wheel, as if his might and his will could prevent the unpreventable.

In that slowed down version of reality that happens during accidents, she saw the elk's eyes roll white with terror before it bounded away, seemingly unharmed though she could have sworn the truck glanced off of it.

Elk saved, the truck was sliding, so slowly its movement seemed benign. It went sideways across the road, the nose pointed to a steep embankment. The driver's side tire slipped over, and then hers followed. For a single second the truck hung suspended, and then it lurched, the front end plowed into hard ground, and they stopped hard.

Lila, pushed forward against the dash, her nose nearly on the windshield, was afraid to even breathe in case it sent the truck cascading farther down the embankment.

"Are you okay?"

His voice was deep, his calm could be reassuring if she was inclined to let it be.

She nodded, still afraid to move.

"We're hung up. Don't worry." Dead calm, a man who dealt well with calamity.

"D-d-don't worry?" she stammered. "We're hanging by a thread. We're in the middle of nowhere. We're in the middle of a blizzard. It's almost dark."

"Uh-huh."

He wasn't getting the seriousness of their predicament.

"We're out of cell phone range!" she told him, and could hear the squeaky note of panic in her own voice.

And then he laughed.

She was not sure she had ever heard a more reassuring

sound—his easy laughter surely meant they were not in as much danger as she thought they were in.

Though his laughter—bold, deep, full of life—awakened her to a danger of a different kind. She pulled back from where she was squished up against the dashboard of the truck and peeked at him.

This was the man she had glimpsed in his hint of a smile a long time ago.

Extraordinary. Something beyond handsome. Deep. Capable. A man who handled what life threw at him with a certain ruggedly appealing confidence in his own abilities and strengths.

"It's not as bad as you think it is," he told her. "Here put your arms around my neck."

If it hadn't been as bad as she thought it was before she put her arms around his neck, it certainly was after.

She was not just aware of his strength, of the steady beat of his heart as he lifted her easily from the truck.

No, she was aware of the heavily falling snow, and the deep silence, and the fact the light was now leeching from the air, even though it was barely four o'clock. She was also aware that truck was not going anywhere. They were stranded in a world of snow and cold and elements. A world as foreign to her as if she had journeyed to a brand-new and menacing land.

She was aware she was now totally reliant on him.

And that if there was ever a man a woman should be grateful for being totally reliant on, it was this one.

He set her down on the steep pitch of the bank, looked her up and down, hard, then reached in and pulled Boo from the truck.

The danger of her situation deepened, because Boo

reached up and licked at the bottom of her rescuer's chin. And for a moment in Brody's face she saw an unguarded tenderness so lovely it took her breath away.

"How long," he said, deliberate casualness in his voice, "until someone misses you?"

Her aunt and obviously her uncle had known she was going for the tree today. But she doubted that either of them would check to see if she had arrived home. Her aunt had done that at first, checked in on her, knowing how nervous she could be at night.

But as the hometown feeling of Snow Mountain had wrapped around her, as comfy as a favorite blanket, Lila had asked her to stop.

Would anyone notice the tree had not appeared in the square on schedule? The grand reopening was still days away. She doubted it.

"It could be a while," she said. "You?"

"Same. I'm on days off. Not scheduled to work again until Monday night."

The same. She understood just how much the same they were. Alone in a world of couples and families. Alone. No one to miss them if they didn't get back home right away. It was Saturday, no one would miss them for close to forty-eight hours.

And how exactly did a person like that, *alone,* write a book about how to have a perfect Christmas? she asked herself morosely. She was wanting to think about something like that, suddenly a *small* concern, rather than the harsh reality of the predicament they were in. Already, she missed the warmth she had so enjoyed inside the cab of the truck. The snow, driven by wind, stung her face.

"The upside is no one will be worried unnecessarily,"

he said easily, as if the swiftly deepening cold and night did not bother him one little bit.

"Excuse me if I don't exactly see that as an upside."

That smile again, reassuring, strong. "The guys will be really busy with a storm like this. I wouldn't want a whole bunch of manpower diverted to rescuing us when we don't need rescuing."

"We don't?"

"No. There's a hunter's cabin not far from here. It will be stocked with emergency supplies. We'll hole up there for the night. In the morning, I'll walk out. Did you see that farm we passed on the way up here? Bryce Hampton's place. He'll have a tractor. He can pull the truck out."

A night in a cabin. With a man whose laughter sounded like that. With a man who looked as if he would die protecting her if he had to. She refused to give in to her awareness of his lips, his *presence,* the thought that they were going to be alone, and that there was something between them that was so strong she was not sure she could fight it.

Instead she forced herself to think disciplined thoughts. *A cabin.* She latched on to it desperately. Maybe she could put a chapter on Christmas vacations in her book. Cabins: cozy fires, mulled wine, a popcorn string for the tree.

While she immersed herself in fantasy—always a safe defense from reality—Brody saw what he could salvage from the truck: the thermos, a few leftover cookies, the blanket, his chain saw.

Her ability to convince herself it was all a grand adventure, an opportunity to experience an alternate Christmassy locale, lasted about three minutes. Even the undeniable sensuality of the man faded into the background. Lila dismissed her fantasies and focused on the tasks at hand. Trying to get back up the incline was nearly impossible.

She fell and her mittens got wet, and Brody insisted she brush all the snow off her clothes before they moved again. Then he had to shove her from behind to get her up over the lip onto the road. At least she wasn't the only one struggling. She noticed Boo making a terrible gasping sound.

It seemed she was struggling endlessly through snow and darkness. In no time, she was exhausted, cold and hungry. She had tripped and fallen over logs and rocks hidden by snow at least a dozen times. Each time he had patiently helped her up, brushed her off, encouraged her. This was an amazing side to him that made her think—as if the ground she was on was not treacherous enough—he would make such a good father.

"Are you sure you know where the cabin is?" Her hands were so cold, the mittens like clumps of ice at the end of her sleeves. And the fabric of her jeans, frozen solid even though he had painstakingly brushed the snow from them after each fall, felt as if it was burning her legs.

What if he didn't know where the cabin was? How could anyone really know where it was? All the trees looked the same. They had left the road behind long ago. What if he was leading them farther and farther from safety? What if—

"I know where the cabin is." A voice a person could believe in. The kind of voice that instilled confidence in desperate situations. But then, that was what he was trained to do. Deal with crises. Car accidents. Bank robberies. Protests.

He could be *pretending,* she decided. He was making her go ahead of him, and she turned to scan his face.

Absolutely calm. A face incapable of any kind of pretense.

"Just a few more minutes," he said.

"I need a rest."

"No." He said it just like that, no gentleness this time. The firmness of a whip cracking. In other circumstances she might have resented his high-handedness, but she recognized this situation needed a leader, and he was it.

She cast one more glance back at him. When had he picked up the dog? He was carrying everything now: the basket, the blanket, the chain saw, the dog. And she was complaining?

"Move it," he said.

It was when she heard that tone of voice, entirely no nonsense, expecting obedience—as if their lives depended on it—that she understood he'd protected her all along from the precariousness of the position they were in.

When she really did not think she could go another slippery step down that path of snow booby-trapped roots and fallen logs, a shape loomed black and square against the darkness of the night.

How could she feel so painfully disappointed?

Because part of what had kept her going was her idea of a cabin: welcoming porch, golden logs, a chimney. A place a family might gather to enjoy a simpler Christmas and each other.

What was ahead of them was so obviously a shack.

She wanted to cry. Because it just underscored what he had said earlier. She had a problem with fantasy.

Still, when he shoved in the door and shut it behind them the space was nothing except unrelentingly black. It was at least as cold inside as it had been outside.

"What is that smell?" she asked weakly.

"Mice. Pack rats." He set down the dog, thudded into something and swore softly, but a moment later a lamp flickered to life and she saw the cabin in its humble entirety.

Most importantly, at the center of the single room, there was a stove, black and potbellied, with some wood stacked beside it.

But other than that welcome sight, the cabin was a horror: unpainted plywood floor and walls. No windows. A two-by-four single shelf, plywood, close to the floor, that she realized without enthusiasm was the bed. An old table was in the center of the room, flanked by two stump chairs. There was a plank countertop covered in white powder.

"Mice have been in the flour," he said matter-of-factly.

Mice in the flour. Some Christmas story that would make.

She turned and looked at him in the flickering light, and felt ashamed of herself. She had complained, but he was the one who was not dressed warmly, who had carried everything the whole way. This place might not be her fantasy, but the reality was it would help them survive a very bad night, and fairly comfortably, too.

His cheeks were becoming faintly whisker darkened, the snow melted in his hair and on the collar of his jacket.

His hands were bare.

"Your hands must be freezing," she said. "I had mittens on and mine are still cold."

"I'm okay."

He showed her, by reaching for her hands. He plucked her mittens off, one at a time, placed her hands between the amazing warmth of his.

She closed her eyes against the sensation: her whole world became not the storm outside, not the mice in the flour, but *this*. Warmth. Strength. Something to hold on to.

"I'm a terrible sissy," she said. "A liability. I'm sorry. I've never been lost in the wilderness before. I've never actually seen snow before. Except when I was ten. I remember it being *fun*. Not miserable."

There was a terrible catch in her voice. How could she ever write a book about Christmas now that she knew the truth: snow had a downside. It caused accidents. It caused loss of feeling to limbs.

"You were a trooper," he said, as if he really meant it, and then let go of her hands. "I was born doing this kind of stuff. And as dramatic as it sounds, I'm afraid we were never lost in the wilderness. My brother and I knew these mountains like the backs of our hands."

"I didn't know you had a brother."

He moved away from her, adjusted the lamp, moved with easy efficiency to the stove.

"In about five minutes," he said, ignoring her attempt at small talk, "you'll want to open the door, it will be so warm in here. It's amazing how a little heater like this can warm a small space."

And it did. But what she was newly amazed at was *him*. Taking each challenge in his stride, getting the fire going, checking the supplies. Soon he had a pot filled with snow heating on the stove, another bubbling with something that smelled so good.

He fed the dog some of the tinned stew he'd found in one of the cupboards, found a mattress rolled up tight against the mice, unfolded it and found bedding stored in tightly closed plastic boxes.

After he'd fed her and the warmth was creeping steadily

into her very bones, Lila realized she was actually starting to feel *happy* to be here. A funny kind of euphoria began to fill her up. A delayed gratitude for survival, she assumed.

"You know what's weird?" she said almost to herself. "I feel really safe. Isn't that crazy?"

"We were never in danger," he told her, giving her a quizzical look.

But she realized she felt as if she had been in danger for a long time, had lived with the finely held tension of one who had been hunted, and who could never forget what it meant to be prey.

Except here. Without any locks on the door, seemingly a million miles from any other human being, the snow wrapping her in a cocoon of security.

It occurred to her that even if it was irrational, she felt totally safe, really and truly safe, for the first time in two years. It occurred to her that not feeling safe, all those nights of listening, *waiting,* had exhausted her almost beyond comprehension. No wonder, she thought almost sleepily, that she hadn't been able to write a book!

It was a wonder she'd been able to open her store, organize the SOS committee.

No wonder her thoughts about Brody were confused, and out of control. No wonder she didn't know from one minute to the next what she wanted.

She was perpetually exhausted. She felt her gaze drift longingly to that uncomfortable-looking bed.

And then it occurred to her there were two of them and a single bed, and she was not safe at all.

And her sense of euphoria did not ease, not even one little bit.

* * *

The gods had it in for him. Brody Taggert knew that for sure. Because here he was, in a remote mountain cabin, with the woman he had sworn was the most dangerous to him, the one human being on earth he most had to stay away from.

Because of how he had felt for that moment after he had told her about the Murphy girl. The burden lightened.

Because of how he had felt when the truck started to slide, and as they had walked through the cold night here: as if he would lay down his life for her, without one thought, *gladly*.

Because of how he had felt, really, from the first moment he had met her, as if his world was tilting.

And mostly because of how he felt right now.

Strangely contented to be with her. Of course, being out here, far away from the trappings of civilization, had always had that effect on him. Soothed something in him. Made him aware of something bigger running the show.

So why had he not come here with his grief?

Because these places had always belonged to him and his brother *together*. He with his rifle, Ethan with his sketchbook.

He had thought he would feel nothing but pain returning to the places that had been theirs together, alone.

But he was not alone. And for a reason he could not fathom, he was not resentful of Lila's presence in this place that had been so special to him and Ethan.

He snorted at his philosophical turn. The truth about his contentment had not a thing to do with philosophy. He had been handed a bad situation, and was making the best of it. He had found them shelter from a storm that was going to get a lot nastier before it abated. That was something to feel grateful for. Lila had always made him feel protective, and now he was protecting her, and it was strangely satisfying.

Of course, in a few minutes the thing she was most

going to need protecting from was himself, since he was about to get Lila Grainger out of her jeans.

Okay, not in the way that a man usually thought of that.

Then again, he had a feeling things with Lila Grainger would probably never go quite the way a man thought they should or would.

He had fed her, and now she was drinking tea. The color was returning to her hands, and there was an expression of peace on her face that made him wish he could capture moments with a pencil, as Ethan had.

A few strokes of pencil or charcoal, and a moment saved forever. Brody had books full of those etchings at home, put away in boxes that he never opened.

But suddenly he felt ready to look at them again, to see the world through his brother's eyes.

Lila shivered, despite the warmth of the fire, and he knew she was never going to be warm as long as she had on those soaked jeans.

"Uh, you're going to have to take those pants off," he said.

She shot him a look, hugged her tea a little tighter, pretended she hadn't heard him.

"I'll turn my back. Here's the blanket from the picnic. It's dry now. Your pants aren't."

"What about yours?" she asked. "They must be wet, too."

"Damp. I didn't do quite as much rolling around in the snow as you. I'll be okay."

He passed her the blanket and turned his back, acting as if he expected to be obeyed, but he was still pleasantly surprised when she muttered, "Okay," and he turned around to find her with the blanket wrapped around her like a long skirt, the jeans in a puddle at her feet.

He picked them up, hung them deliberately by the fire,

trying not to notice how small they were, how straight: every curve they had appeared to have as he walked behind them had been added by her.

"Since I'm in the embarrassing position of having no pants, I guess now would be a good time to ask my most embarrassing question. Where's the bathroom?"

"Uh." It was his turn to blush.

The bathroom? Every tree was a bathroom to a guy. In hunting season, there was a log over a pit toilet behind here.

For the more delicate, he just wasn't sure. Especially now that he'd gotten her out of her pants. He didn't want to send her out into the snow with the blanket. That would get wet, too, and she was just starting to warm up.

"How would you feel about using a bucket?" he asked.

"Like I'd rather die first," she answered, and set down the tea with an accusing look as if he was personally responsible for the primitive lack of facilities.

"I won't think any less of you," he said uneasily. "I don't have any problems with bodily functions."

The wrong thing to say, obviously. She glared at him.

"Look," he said, struck by inspiration, "think of it as camping. Haven't you ever been camping?"

"No."

"Didn't you ever want to go?"

"We have alligators in Florida!"

"We have cabins with no plumbing in Washington," he said. "Life is full of hazards."

"I know that," she said somberly, and he thought of the locks on her door, the *incident* she had referred to when she had felt that first shiver of fear.

"I know you do. I do, too." He handed her the bucket. "I'll go outside. You might as well get it over with."

"When I write my book about creating the perfect Christmas, this is not making it into the chapter on Christmas cabins."

The dog, her stomach unsettled from the unfamiliar food, chose that moment to make a sound like air being released from a balloon.

"And neither is that," she said.

And then they were both laughing, and despite the unexpected twists and turns of life, he was aware it was the first time in a long time he had laughed like that. And it felt good, as if something that had been empty inside of him was filling up.

CHAPTER SIX

WARM. Safe. Cozy. Happy.

The snow fell unabated outside the cabin, Lila could hear the wind howling under the eaves.

But inside was only warmth. It was like the end to a perfect Christmas story, even though they were in a place with no tree, no lights, no turkey. There was a *feeling* in here, in this humble cabin, and it was exactly the feeling she'd been trying to create when she had started *Miss L. Toe* as an Internet business, and again when she had decided to open a storefront. It was exactly the feeling that she had wanted to create when she had agreed to write that book.

It was a feeling of being home.

Ridiculous to feel that way. No electricity. No plumbing. Not a single luxury or amenity.

And yet sitting at that small table, wearing a blanket, the dog on top of her feet, Brody Taggert dealing cards, that's how she felt.

Home.

It was because of him. Because he was a man you could come home to.

She snuck a look at him over the top of her cards, felt her breath stop. In the flickering, imperfect light of the lantern, he looked gorgeous, and faintly roguish with his whisker-roughened chin and cheeks.

"I've never seen anyone cheat at crib before," he said, throwing down his cards, stretching. His shirt lifted way up. She could see the taut line of his tummy.

"I didn't cheat!"

"You don't get three for a pair."

She looked down at the board, realized she had been so engrossed in all his taut lines, she might have taken the extra point. Since she wasn't about to admit that, she said, "Show me the rule book!"

"Why bother? You're the type that reads the rule book and then just does whatever you want anyway."

"How would you know that on our brief acquaintance?"

He lifted his eyebrows at her. She wished he wouldn't do that. In the flickering light it made him look wickedly sexy. In this primitive cabin it was easy to picture him as a renegade highwayman or a pirate. Rugged enough to make his own rules.

"Anatomy of a protest," he pointed out, reminding her he was on the *right* side of the law. "You knew you needed a permit."

"It was going to take weeks! It was for a good cause."

"Precisely my point. I bet you think winning at crib is a good cause, too."

"Right up there with saving Christmas trees," she said passionately.

He smiled. Something in him had relaxed. Surrendered. Something in her had relaxed, surrendered.

"What made you become a policeman?" she asked, wanting to take advantage of this moment of surrender to *know* him. "I can picture you as a renegade."

"You can, hmm?" That smile deepened wickedly.

Visions of the highwayman became more clear. "I'm afraid I can," she admitted, "Quite clearly."

"I was a renegade when I was younger. Mostly mischief. Garden raiding, stealing mailboxes from the ends of driveways. But for a while it escalated. Some pretty hard drinking, fighting. I came to in a cell one morning, with Hutch sitting in the bunk across from me, waiting for me to wake up.

"I'd gotten tanked up the night before, hit one of his guys. I didn't even remember it."

"That's pretty serious, isn't it?" she asked.

"You're not kidding. Assault on a police officer? Given the fact I had collected a string of drunk and disorderlies by then, I knew a judge was not going to take pity on me."

"What happened?"

His face softened. "Hutch said he figured I was at a crossroads, a place where the choices I made were going to affect the rest of my life. He told me he'd been watching me. If I was going to choose a side, he wanted me on his side. And, instead of charging me, he threw down an application for the police department.

"It was a lifeline. And a turning point." He looked suddenly embarrassed, a man not used to talking about himself.

Sitting across from him, Lila could see exactly what her uncle had seen: integrity, honor, strength, but coupled with an almost amazing lack of ego. Even in a kid getting in trouble, all those qualities would have shone through.

"That's the kind of man your uncle is," he said gruffly. "That's why I'd do just about anything for him."

"Including go find a Christmas tree with his niece?"

"Yeah," he said with a small grin, "even that."

And then, a man who felt he had said way too much about himself, he got up from the table, and the next question hung in the air between them.

What now? Where was it going?

"Where are we sleeping?" she asked. It came out sounding faintly breathless, excited, hopeful.

"You can have the bed. Boo and I will take the floor." Every quality her uncle had ever seen in him was clearly visible now. Integrity, honor, strength. And he was going to use them all to fight the attraction, to be the man who could be trusted with another man's niece.

Even with the little wood heater cranked up to full blast, she could feel the chill rising up through the floor. They had the picnic blanket that she was wrapped in and two wool blankets that had been in the cabin, thin and frayed at the edges. He would need those both if he was going to be on that floor. She shivered at the thought.

"We could share the bed." She was glad for the light in here, because maybe it hid the stain that moved up her cheeks.

"No, we couldn't."

"Why not?" She told herself she was not suggesting they sleep together, not in an intimate way, only that they share the few comforts there were in the cabin. But she knew something in her was ready for more, hoping for more.

How much more? She was not going to find out.

"Boo snores," he said, deadpan.

But she knew that wasn't it. She knew that kiss outside his barn, a kiss he had bestowed on her in a fury, was in this room with them, and had been there, right below the surface, from the moment they had gotten in that truck cab together.

She licked her lips as if his taste lingered there, and somehow, even though it was weeks later, it felt as if it did.

He looked at her, his gaze brooding, simmering with passion that she wanted desperately to explore.

She got up, too, leaned toward him.

He took a step back, but he could not hide the reluctance with which he stepped back. He whistled to the dog, glanced once more at her lips and then turned on his heel and went outside.

A whoosh of cold air and snow blew in the door behind him.

She could wait for him. She could tempt him. But the truth was, she did not have that kind of confidence in herself or in her judgment. The pleasant exhaustion that she had been feeling almost from the moment she came in that door enveloped her now in a lethargy she could not fight.

Lila went to the bed, rearranged her blanket around herself, lay down on the lumpy mattress. Despite the fact it smelled of something—she hoped not mice—she could not keep her eyes open for even one second.

A moment later he came in from outside, shook the snow off himself, took off his boots. They thudded to the floor, she imagined his bare feet, but did not give in to the temptation to look at them. More rustling, his shirt whispering to the floor. That proved more temptation than she could handle.

She opened her eyes, but she had barely seen him—the ridges and lines of pure and intoxicating male beauty—when he blew out the lamp.

Blackness more complete than she had ever experienced enveloped her.

She heard him arranging the thin blankets on the floor, crawl in between them, the dog settling in beside him.

She could hear his breathing; it was all that prevented complete panic at the sudden impenetrable darkness.

"It's really dark in here," she whispered, trying to keep the wobble from her voice.

"Mmm."

"Really dark. I've never been in a room this dark in my whole life. I'm holding up my hand, I can't even see it."

Silence, and then softly. "Are you scared of the dark, Miss Lila Toe?"

His voice in the darkness, so soft, teasing her, using an endearment, was the same as his voice in a storm, a sound someone could hold on to, that could make them feel safe in a world that just wasn't.

"It's just there's always a streetlight," she said, avoiding his question. "Some kind of light. From the hallway. Or the bathroom."

"You're scared of the dark," he concluded, his voice without recrimination.

"Maybe a little," she admitted.

"Have you always been like that?"

It was her turn to hesitate. How vulnerable did she want to be to him? "No."

"Maybe you should tell me about *the incident*. Tell me what happened."

Suddenly the darkness made it feel safe to tell him, she *wanted* to. And so she told him, detail by detail.

"I was just starting *Miss L. Toe* as an Internet business. My love of all things Christmas had just been a hobby up until that point, so I was still working full-time as a research writer for a big marketing company. A new guy joined our department—Ken Whittaker."

Lila told Brody about Ken's growing but unwanted

interest in her, her trying to be polite and then having to be firm. The more she said no, the more he came at her: roses, invitations, poetry left on her desk.

"They finally fired him after he filled up every drawer in my desk with confetti," she said. "It was apparent to everyone it wasn't a harmless crush. He was harassing me. It triggered rage in him, as if I was responsible for the fact he'd been fired. The notes and poems kept coming, to my house, to work, but they turned nasty. He was in his car outside the office, outside my apartment building. Then one time I went for dinner with friends, and he broke into my apartment and stole some of my things. I finally got a restraining order."

"And it made everything worse," Brody guessed softly.

"How did you know?"

"It's one of the most frustrating crimes for a cop to deal with, stalking. In the worst cases, it seems like every attempt to control it just deepens the obsession, the rage, makes everything worse."

"Worse doesn't describe it." She stopped talking for a moment, took a deep shuddering breath. "He broke into my house. At night. I woke up with him hovering over top of me with a knife. He held me at knifepoint in my own kitchen for six hours."

Brody swore softly in the dark.

"He was raging and then crying and then raging again. To this day, I don't know what stopped him from raping me. Or killing me. Twice he held the knife against my neck so hard he drew blood."

"What did you do?"

She hesitated. "Lied my head off. Told him I loved him. Told him I wanted to spend the rest of my life with him. Told him—" her voice cracked "—I wanted to have his babies."

"Good instincts," Brody said approvingly.

"Afterward, when I thought about it, I felt sick that I had said things like that to him. Things that should be so sacred."

"They kept you alive. In my book that probably qualifies as sacred."

She was quiet, contemplating that. "A neighbor happened to be walking by. There was a back walkway past my apartment that went to the garbage. She was taking her trash out and happened to glance in my window.

"Later she told me she was only taking it out because she'd had fish the night before. Her garbage wasn't full. My life was probably saved because my neighbor had fish. Imagine. Amazing."

"I guess that qualifies as sacred, too," he said, his voice low and reassuring in the blackness of the night.

"It's why I moved to Snow Mountain. The Internet business was doing great, I had an advance on writing a book on Christmas that could get me started here, but the real reason was even after Ken was convicted, I couldn't stay there anymore. It seemed like the fear, the terror had seeped into the walls. I had to get to someplace new, I had to find something I could believe in."

"Christmas?" he guessed, and she could hear the calm in his voice, the evenness of his breathing. She thought she could hear acceptance, as if he did not for one minute blame her, the way she had blamed herself.

"Christmas," she said softly. "Or maybe what it stands for—peace, people loving one another, a time of miracles." She hesitated and then continued, "Maybe I'm looking for one myself, because when I moved I realized that the fear hadn't just seeped into the walls of my apartment. It had seeped into me."

"What miracle are you looking for, Lila?"

And it was the easiest thing in the world to trust him, which made her think maybe her miracle had already started to happen.

"I want to not be afraid anymore, to not have the knot in my stomach, to not startle at every loud noise. I want to be who I was before. And from the moment I walked in the door of this cabin, that's how I felt."

And suddenly, the exhaustion of two years of feeling that tension caught up with her.

"I want to sleep again, Brody. For a whole night. To not keep waking up with my heart pounding so loud in my ears it sounds like footsteps coming toward me."

"Lila?"

"Mmm-hmm?"

"You go ahead and sleep like that. I've got your back."

I've got your back. That was what she had not felt for a long, long time. As if she was not alone. Protected.

Amazingly, she buried her nose in the world's smelliest mattress and slept instantly for the first time in forever.

Brody lay awake, listening to the sound of her steadily deepening breathing, contemplating the killing fury he felt at a man who was already taken care of, supposedly paying his debt to Lila and society. But it seemed to Brody no matter how many years the perpetrator spent in jail he would never be able to fix what he had done to Lila.

Brody dealt with creeps. It would probably bug Lila to know that. Yup. They were everywhere. Even in Snow Mountain. He was always clinical in how he treated them, his personal feelings controlled, not an issue.

Now he realized he was a man capable of murder.

If that guy, Ken, got out and came after her, because they always came after the object of their obsession. They never quit until someone was dead. Brody knew he'd look after it. That simple.

The floor was hard and cold. He was uncomfortable and that was good. It kept his mind off all that softness just a few feet away. It kept his mind off the fact that when she had asked where they were going to sleep, he thought he'd detected the faintest hint of an invitation.

Brody was determined to be the guy Hutch thought he was, all those years ago when he'd given him a chance.

After what seemed to be a long, long time, Boo's breathing raspy in his ears, Brody fell asleep.

And woke to the sound of whimpering.

Not Boo's, either.

The whimpering intensified to a frightened cry, and he was already up by the time she started screaming.

"Get off of me! Get off!" Her voice had a hysterical edge, and Brody leaped toward the bed, tried to locate the source of her distress in the blackness.

Because of his last thoughts before sleep, he was ready to do murder in her defense if he had to.

But that was probably why the dream had come to her, too. Her last thoughts, thinking she was free of all that terror, hoping to be free, but her subconscious not quite ready to let go.

His eyes adjusted to the darkness. Lila was struggling under the weight of…his dog.

He bent and quickly lifted the dog off her. "Hey, it's okay. It was just Boo. She must have gotten cold."

Or she couldn't stay away. His dog was in love with

Lila, it was obvious, and Boo didn't have to control her attraction to people the way he did.

But Lila was beyond the point where she could be rational. She began to sob, punching away at an invisible enemy, her arms hopelessly tangled in the blanket, which seemed to be adding to her panic.

Brody hesitated, not knowing how strong he was. But then he decided to be strong enough to do what she needed done, not what was safest for him.

Because what he did was not safe at all.

He sat down on the edge of her bed and pulled her body, wrapped tight like a sausage, into his lap.

He loosened the blanket around her, her arms free, she flailed at him, and he let her flail, her blows landing harmlessly on his naked chest.

"It's all right," he said over and over, making no attempt to capture her hands. "No one's ever going to hurt you again, Lila. Never."

Slowly the panic subsided from her, the punches to his chest grew weaker. The sobs further apart and then soft, like a beaten puppy crying.

"Hey," he said, "hey, it's okay. He can't hurt you anymore. I won't let him."

At those words she finally stilled, took a long, deep breath, relaxed against him. He could feel her tears sliding, molten, down his skin.

"Brody?"

"Yeah, it's me."

"Sorry, I didn't mean to hurt you. I didn't know it was you. Even after you told me, all I could feel was panic. I'm sorry. I feel like an idiot."

"You didn't hurt me. You don't have anything to be

sorry about. It takes a long, long time for some wounds to heal. Some never do."

"Do you have a wound that's never healed, Brody?"

He could feel something catching in his throat and it took him a long time to answer. When he did, he said only, "I think everyone does."

She sighed her agreement against him, her breath warmer than fire on his chest.

"That's why I sleep with the light on. Not just the bathroom one, the one beside my bed, too."

"I can put the lantern on if you want."

She sighed, again. "It's okay. Brody, lie down beside me. The floor's cold."

He heard something else. She needed to be held. Maybe she needed to know a man could hold her without hurting her.

He lay her down on the bed, she scooted way over against the wall. He lay down beside her, stiffly, not wanting to touch her, not having any idea how much testing he could take.

She snuggled into him, laid her head once more on the nakedness of his chest. He hesitated and put his arm around the slenderness of her shoulders, tugged her into his side.

"Brody, will you kiss me?"

He knew all the reasons he shouldn't. All of them. He knew she was his boss's niece, and this couldn't go well.

He knew that he had so little to give, all the best parts of him buried with his brother, the part of him that might have been willing to risk again slowly shutting down since Boo had gotten sicker and sicker.

He knew she had come to trust and rely on him because of the situation they were in. He knew this could be temporary. A form of transference. As a first responder, he knew how desperately people could cling to their rescuer, he knew the strength of the bond that could be formed in those terrible seconds of crises.

He knew that after what she had been through, a man who was a cop—a professional defender and rescuer— could seem bigger than life to her, the ideal man, a hero, not a living, breathing person with lots of problems and baggage of his own.

He knew all this, but he also knew this was the limit he had asked to be shown; this, then, was how much testing he could take.

He took her lips in his, he didn't taste them, he drank them. He drank the heady wine of wild strawberries.

"Oh," she breathed against him. "Oh."

"I've wanted to kiss you like this ever since I kissed you like *that*," he admitted huskily.

And then he took her lips again, tenderly, and felt her welcoming answer, as if she had lived her whole life for this moment. Her lips parted beneath his, he felt the sweet curves of her body pressing against his, and he ached for that soft, soft world he had left so far behind him.

But that moment of surrender, of pure bliss was short.

Boo, left on the floor, jumped up on top of them. He tried to catch her, but Boo determined was a dog possessed. She scrambled and wriggled and wheezed her way right in between them. He was hanging on to the narrow bed by a thread, Lila was shoved up against the wall. Boo moaned her delight at having managed to occupy the tiny space between them.

"I think the chaperone has arrived," she said dryly, and then giggled.

Thank God, he thought. He reached past Boo, and touched Lila's cheek, still wet with tears.

When her lips found his fingers, he withdrew them.

She was in no frame of mind to be making decisions like the one he had very nearly asked of her. She was vulnerable. She needed protection, not someone who would take advantage of her.

His strength came back to him. He reached down and grabbed the blankets off the floor, tucked them around her, and around himself, and around Boo, the living, slobbering, snoring bolster.

"Let's go to sleep," he said.

He knew he had made the right decision when she did not argue with him, or press him to get Boo out of the bed.

She wasn't ready.

And God knew, neither was he.

Uncomfortable, but warm at least, he noticed her fragrance had released like a night blooming rose.

"What scent do you wear?" he asked her, when it tickled his nostrils, when he breathed it deep, even though he knew he was teasing himself.

"Scent?"

"Perfume."

"I don't wear perfume. I have sensitive skin. I even have to use unscented bath and laundry soap."

He contemplated that for a moment. All these weeks he'd *imagined* that she smelled like that? Like that last day with his brother? Summer sunshine, the fragrance of the damp woods and strawberries, their hands red with the juice, not eating a single one. Laughing at each find, a way to make amends to their mom for the broken cranberry glass vase.

In the dark of the cabin, with his eyes closed, he could see Ethan, his head thrown back in laughter, his quiet intensity as he sketched the wild strawberry plant.

He shook the vision away. He shook away the thought that the scent of wild strawberries was some kind of gift from his brother. Like a benediction on this woman he shared the darkness of this cabin with on a snowy night.

Ethan had thought like that: he had used his imagination like a bridge to spirit. Ethan had believed in larger purposes and signs from heaven.

Brody had not and did not.

No, he didn't have that good an imagination. She must eat strawberry candy or burn candles or use a strawberry shampoo, something that infused her with that fragrance. There was a logical explanation for why she smelled the way she did.

But he wasn't going to ask her.

He was tired. It had been a long, eventful day. He'd been woken from a deep sleep. A man's thoughts went strange places in the deepest part of the night.

"Good night," he said firmly. "Good night, Lila."

CHAPTER SEVEN

LILA woke to her nose feeling frozen, but unbelievable and delicious warmth everywhere else. The three of them, Brody, Boo and her were squished together in a bed made for one. Sometime in the night she had turned toward him, her hand had snaked by Boo and rested on Brody's shoulder. She let it linger there, awed by how right it felt to be touching him so intimately.

His skin was warm, smooth, resilient under her touch. Just beneath it, she could feel pure muscle, powerful, even when relaxed in sleep.

She looked at his face, and allowed herself the luxury of studying the fullness of his lips, the impossible length and tangle of his lashes, the stubble that darkened the lines of his cheeks and chin, making them seem harder and more pronounced, intimidating, and beautifully masculine.

She shivered. The air in the cabin was cold, making her snuggle deeper under the blankets.

No wonder it was cold in here. Now that morning had come, light was seeping through all the places the cabin was not sealed. There was frost on the wall behind her.

With a smile, she contemplated the fact that after the dream, she had slept until morning.

It had been a long, long time since she'd slept deeply. Until the night in his cabin, every sound had startled her awake, even the furnace whispering on, a cat outside, a branch scraping the window. She would come awake holding her breath, listening, her heart pounding, her hands clammy with fear. Sometimes she awoke, terrified, to such silence she would wonder if it was the tick of her bedroom clock that had awakened her.

Boo stirred beside her, opened an eye. She could have sworn the dog grinned at the position she found herself in, sandwiched neatly between the warmth of two humans. Lila freed one hand from the blanket, scratched Boo's chest and was rewarded with a slurp from an enormous pink tongue across her face.

She giggled and saw Brody stir, went very still as she watched him come awake. It was as breathtaking a thing to see him wake up as it had been to watch him sleep.

Slowly, a wrinkle in his forehead, his lips moving, then his eyes fluttering. An unconscious stretch of shoulders, and then his eyes opened, and he studied her with sleepy astonishment, a smile tickling the firmness of his lips.

But then he was all the way awake suddenly.

She realized her hand still rested on his shoulder, and she yanked it away, but he leaped from bed, ready for action.

She had caught a quick glance of him without his shirt last night before they had been plunged into darkness, and she had felt the magnificent strength of him as he had held her after she had woken, terrified, with Boo's weight on top of her.

This morning she gave herself over to the study of the perfect male form, just as she had given herself over to the study of his face.

His chest was solid, cut-marble perfection, the column of his throat, joining it, looked powerful. Then the mounding of pecs, the skin so taut over his rib cage that she could count the ridges there. The broadness tapered to a flat, hard stomach, more ridges, the stunning sexiness of his naked belly button, of his hip bones—just barely—holding up his jeans.

His flesh was completely stippled in goose bumps in seconds, and his nipples hardened to pebbles.

But he acted impervious to the cold, ran a hand through the tousled dark silk of his hair, squatted by the fire.

"I can't believe I let it go out." He began to feed wood into the fire. When the flames flickered healthily, he yanked on his shirt, whistled for the dog without doing up the buttons, shoved his bare feet into his boots, grabbed the water pot and went out the door.

He had barely glanced at her, and she couldn't think of anything that would be more humiliating than the strength of the attraction she felt for him not being reciprocated.

But she was pretty sure, her intuition intact for the first time in years, that he hadn't looked at her precisely because of what he was feeling—a pull as strong as the one she felt.

She wanted to stay in bed forever, or at least until the cabin was warmer, but she felt so invigorated. The woman she had been yesterday coming up the mountain, tired, frightened, that woman was gone.

She felt utterly rested, and with that feeling came a sense of clarity she had not enjoyed for so long.

She was glad she was here. She was glad she was here with him.

She got up and squeezed the legs of the pants he had hung up for her last night. They were dry, but still very cold when she put them on and did up the zipper.

By the time he returned, she had sorted through a number of cans and come up with breakfast. She used an ancient can opener to open a can and pour it into a pan.

"You won't believe this," she said, glancing at him, glancing again when she saw he had still not done up the shirt. She made herself look at the mess in the frying pan. "I found bacon for breakfast. Did you know bacon comes in cans?"

He stood there for a moment watching her, giving himself over to watching her as he had not done earlier, and then he motioned for her. "Come see this," he said.

He opened the door and they stood together on the porch and she felt her heart swell.

Not because he stood so close to her they were nearly touching, but because they were touching in a new way as they shared this sight together.

He had wanted her to see it. He had needed to share this with her.

Man created elves in parks and Santas who waved, man created beautiful homes and lovely gardens, and cities and paintings and museums.

Man created imitations of beauty.

Because looking out over the snow-covered world outside that cabin, her throat closed. They had come from the back of the cabin the night before, through the trees, in darkness. But today she could clearly see the cabin was located at the top of a sloping mountain meadow. The view was panoramic: mountain ridges folding in on themselves, a distant lake, a farm way down there in the valley, a thin plume of smoke coming out the chimney of the house.

The snow had stopped during the night and the world was blanketed in a sea of mounding white. The morning sun was coming out, tinged in pink, and it sparked off the snow as if thousands and thousands of tiny diamonds had been sewn onto that cotton-candy blanket. The branches of the trees dipped under the weight of white they carried.

And it was so silent, the world absolutely muted except for the breath of the man who stood next to her, and the crackle of the fire behind them.

She hugged herself against the cold, reluctant to go back inside to where it was warm.

"Is it colder this morning?"

"Always colder when it's clear like this," he said.

She turned to go back inside, but she suddenly saw it wasn't just the view he had brought her out here to show her. No, he was grinning, and nudging something with his toe.

It was a sled so old it could have been in the window of an antique store.

It had steel runners that might have been red once, but that were now rusty, a body shaped like a garden gate lying flat, an old piece of twine attached to the front steering bar.

"Before we go, I want to replace the wood we've used," he told her. "You can try this out."

Go. She didn't want to even think of that.

Yesterday, when they had arrived here, the cabin had not been anything that she had envisioned a cabin being. But today it felt different. As if it had given her gifts she could never repay: the gift of seeing just how little it took in material possessions to feel content. Full. Happy.

The gift of seeing you could put a thousand locks on your door and never feel safe until you had conquered the fear inside of yourself.

And one other unexpected gift: she could tell that he didn't want to leave, either, even if he said they were staying only because he wanted to replace the wood. It was just an excuse. To be here. To enjoy what they had found here just a little longer.

A bit of magic in a world without magic.

A hint of miracles in a humble cabin far, far from the nearest church.

"I think the bacon's burning," he said wryly.

She dashed back into the cabin, turned to see him standing in the open doorway, outlined in radiance by the morning light, the dog at his side.

And a look in his eyes as he watched her that stole her breath as surely as the scene outside the door.

An hour later, Brody stopped and wiped the sweat from his forehead. He had felled a dead tree behind the cabin. There was an unwritten law in these remote places that offered refuge: you left more than you took.

In his younger days he had been careless about such things, but Ethan never had. If his younger brother used one stick of wood, he put back two, if he drank one pouch of hot chocolate from the cabin's emergency supplies, he would bring back a whole box the next time they came.

Brody looked at the tree. He had used the chain saw to limb and section the tree, now he was using an ax that belonged with the cabin to chop the blocks of wood smaller. There would be a least a season's worth of wood here when he was done.

He contemplated the possibility he was a better man than he would have been if he hadn't had Ethan for a brother.

His attention turned to Lila. She was pulling the sled up the hill, yet another time, the dog glued to her heel. Apparently she wasn't going to get bored of that activity, every time she shouted with glee he found himself shaking his head and smiling.

He squinted at Boo.

Whatever was in this place, the dog was benefiting from it, too. Boo was almost puppylike in her joy, shoveling snow with her nose, bouncing, chasing imaginary squirrels, yapping at the heels of the sled.

People sometimes got sick and got better without any medical or scientific explanation.

His dog seemed better—clear-eyed, energetic, eating with more appetite than he'd seen in weeks.

So far Boo had chased the sled down the hill every time, barking with frantic happiness that reflected the shrieks of the woman going down the hill.

Lila was coming toward him now, puffing, a woman on a mission. She radiated joy and confidence, as if the experience of last night, of feeling safe and letting go, had freed her to be who she really was.

For the first time since he had met her, he was aware the faint circles of fatigue were gone from under her eyes.

He could see very clearly what Lila Grainger really was: a woman who vibrated with the life force, who shone with spirit, whose heart had not been broken by her experiences, but made braver.

He took up the ax and swung, cleanly halving a huge block of wood, not unaware of how her eyes rested on him.

Appreciative. *Hungry.* He knew he should not tempt fate by showing off for her, but he did anyway. He reset the halved piece of wood, swung, watched with satisfaction as the ax bit deep into it and it fell in two separate pieces.

"Come down the hill with me," she said. "Just once. Please."

He glanced at the piles of wood mounting around him, and at what was left of the tree. Another hour and he'd be done here. He felt no urgency to leave, despite the fact he had just shown off his strength for her was a clear warning it was time to go.

But they were probably going to have to dig up something to eat before they left now, too. She hadn't realized it, but she was going to have to dry her clothes all over again.

It would be early afternoon before they were ready to go. And that would be if he stayed on task, gathered the split wood, stacked it neatly outside the cabin.

"Please?"

Resist temptation, he ordered himself. So, naturally, he found himself setting down the ax, taking the sled string from her and pulling the sled up to the very top of the hill.

Somehow he was sitting on the front of that sled, his knees nearly touching his ears, and she was on it behind him, pressed so close to him he could feel the beat of her heart through her vest and through his own jacket. Her arms were wrapped around him, her head rested between the broadness of his shoulder blades.

And then they were flying down that hill, the dog racing beside them, the wind stinging his cheeks and making his eyes water.

She was shouting with laughter, and suddenly he was, too. He felt young again, carefree and unburdened, sweetly happy.

The sled veered unexpectedly, he tried to right it, but she threw her weight the wrong way.

He landed in a heap, and she landed with a fierce thump on top of him.

"Amateur," he teased her, choking on snow and laughter.

"Crazy driver," she said, giving his chest an indignant push. Neither of them made any move to, well, move.

He looked up into the laughter of her eyes, the joy on her face and he let himself have it. He let himself have this moment.

Something inside of him let go: his need to protect himself, his need to be in control, his need to not ever be hurt again.

There was a part of him that had decided it would be *wrong* to be happy when his brother was dead. But suddenly, in a moment of illumination, it felt as if it would be more wrong not to be happy, not to grab these unexpected moments of delight and embrace them wholeheartedly.

It suddenly was very clear to him that what would be wrong, what would truly dishonor his brother, would be to not live fully, as fully as he could.

He looked into Lila's shining face and he could clearly see she had risen to the challenge of allowing her heart to be made braver. She was *welcoming* whatever was happening between them.

He let go of his own desire to run from it. If this little chit of a woman could be so brave, then he could be, too.

It was not the kind of bravery that reached into the burning car and pulled out a woman stuck behind the steering wheel. It was not the kind of bravery that went into a dark building with a gun drawn.

It was not the kind of bravery that walked up to a ramshackle house, arms up, rifle pointed out the window at him and said, "Come on, Phil, we've known each other all our lives. Put the rifle down and put the coffee on. We'll talk."

No, it was not that kind of bravery.

That kind of bravery had its place. It was real.

But it did not hold a candle to the kind of bravery that

was being asked of him now. To put his heart at risk. To say *yes* to the mystery of something bigger than he could control. Say yes to what was in the laughter of her eyes, and the way she had rested against his chest last night.

To say yes to life.

He wrapped his arms around her and flipped so that now she was on the bottom and he was on top of her. He straddled her tummy, taking most of his weight on his own knees, but still effectively pinning her. He took a little snow and sprinkled it in her face, and then down the V of delicate skin that showed above her jacket. She struggled and sputtered, and laughed and begged him to stop.

But he didn't. He held her down and then he touched his lips to each place where he had put the snow, took the icy droplets that had melted instantly off her skin.

She went very still beneath him, her eyes wide with discovery, hunger…and welcome. Then he stood up, tugged her up behind him.

Her eyes were locked on his. She licked her lips. She leaned toward him. He leaned toward her.

She stuck a mittful of snow down his pants, and then shrieking with laughter dashed away from him.

They played like young children in the snow, as if they were completely unburdened. They chased each other and buried each other in snow, ran away, got caught on purpose. They made snow angels, and tried riding that sled every way you could ride it: laying down, with her on top of him, her in front, her back against his chest. They even tried riding the sled standing up, as if it were a surfboard. They tumbled off it so often they had snow down their pants and their socks and their jackets. He was pretty sure he had snow in his belly button.

They tasted each other, quick kisses, flitting warmth in the cold. But each stolen kiss, each breathless moment, seemed to last longer than the one before it.

Despite that, and despite the cold of the day, things were heating up.

She was in his arms, nipping at his lips and his ears. "Let's stay here," she said. "Just one more day. The store is closed Mondays, too."

And he didn't work until tomorrow night. Last night it had seemed prudent to stay, a smarter decision than braving the storm and the night for the long walk out to the farm.

"If Marla or Paul have noticed you aren't home, they'll be worried."

"I'm a grown woman!" she said indignantly. "I don't have to check in with anyone."

But he understood that was temptation talking. That was the power of the *thing* in the air between them, because she would never let anyone worry about her, cause distress.

And he understood the temptation. He understood it perfectly. This world was real in a sense: the cold of the snow melting down his neck, the laughter ringing through the quiet meadow, a man's strength and ingenuity being the forces that became most appealing in a world where nothing else mattered. But he understood that this place was insulated from reality, too, like being on a desert island with her.

"Let's go back to the cabin," she said. "We'll make some hot chocolate, dry our clothes, then decide."

But he knew if they made it to that cabin door, hot chocolate was probably going to be the last thing on either of their minds.

He heard it in the distance, and hoped it was not what he thought it was, but he turned to the noise.

"What is that?" she asked of the high-pitched whine that grew louder, desecrating the absolute silence of these high places.

"Look." He pointed. The machines were now visible, flying toward them across the meadow, five of them spread out, leaving a huge V of disrupted snow in their wake.

"What is that?" Lila asked, staring at the approaching machines as if Martians were landing.

"Sleds," he said, and when he saw she didn't understand the slang, he clarified, "Snowmobiles."

"Just when you think you're all alone in the world," she muttered, and he shot her a look at the undisguised resentment in her voice.

"I hope they are not looking for us," he muttered, thinking out loud.

But naturally they were.

And the decision about whether to stay or go was, thankfully or regretfully, taken from his hands.

Just as every other single decision since he had met her had been taken from his hands.

The snowmobiles pulled up, a bunch of local guys, avid sledders. Except for one of them. Hutch probably had not been on a snowmobile since the last time he had used a chain saw. Still, he had been leading the way, and he was first off his machine, unstrapping the helmet, and trying bravely not to look stiff.

"Uncle Paul," Lila said when Hutch's face appeared from under the visor. "What are you doing here?"

But Tag already knew. "You shouldn't have called out rescue," he said, annoyed and embarrassed. "We're okay."

"The snow angels aren't distress signals?" Hutch asked dryly.

Tag actually felt a surge of heat move up his neck.

Hutch was regarding the sled tracks, and the crash sites of messy snow at the bottom of the runs with grave interest.

"You've been sledding?" Hutch finally asked, faintly incredulous.

Tag shrugged, took an interest in moving some snow around with the toes of his boots. "Mostly Lila," he mumbled, like a grade seven boy who'd been caught peeking in the girl's locker room.

"She hasn't seen much snow," he rushed on when Hutch didn't say anything. "That's why we didn't head home as soon as day broke." Did he sound defensive? He sounded defensive. "Of course we didn't know anyone would come looking for us."

"Marla called Lila's place last night to see how it had gone with the tree. She started worrying when she wasn't home. She tried right up until midnight. Then I called your place, thinking—" Hutch glared at him just to know what he had been thinking, and what he would have thought, too, if his assumption of an inappropriate liaison had been correct.

So much for Lila declaring herself an independent adult. Hutch, old-fashioned on points of honor, would make any man who took advantage of her pay and pay dearly.

"When you weren't there, I figured a vehicle problem. The guys were going for a ride anyway, first great snow of the year, so I invited myself along to have a look around. We found the truck up the branch road, followed your tracks. I figured you'd be here. One of you and Ethan's old haunts."

"Whose Ethan?" Lila, who had been silent until that point—who actually looked like she was seething at the interruption—asked.

And Brody realized he really had allowed himself to live

in an insulated world. He could see the look of relief on Hutch's face that she didn't know who Ethan was. His boss assumed it meant nothing had happened, that they barely knew each other at all.

Was that a fair assumption?

He had not told Lila about Ethan. Or Boo. He had kept all his secrets. The snowmobiles had probably arrived in the knick of time.

He turned to Lila. "You go with your uncle," he said. "I'll finish up here. Hutch, if you can get someone to pull the truck out for me, me and Boo will walk out later in the day."

"I'll stay, too," Lila announced.

Which earned her, and him, a quizzical look from her uncle.

"No," Brody said. "I want you to go."

Yesterday, that probably would have made her cry. But she was leaving the victim role far behind her, and now she just looked mad.

He didn't have to fix that. He really didn't. Especially not in front of her uncle, who had started to frown.

"I'll call you," he said, suddenly not caring what her uncle thought. "I'll be home by early afternoon. I'll drop the tree off at the park for you. What are you doing for supper tonight?"

"No plans," she said, beaming at him in a way that he thought women reserved for diamond rings.

A stupid thing, to drag this out, to subject himself to more temptation, to ask her that in front of Hutch, who was glowering at him.

But Tag recognized the truth. He was a strong man, yes, but not strong enough to leave what he had found here on the mountain.

Hope.

A tiny hope had found a crack in his heart and taken up residence there like a spark that could become a flame.

For the first time in six and a half years, Tag was aware he wanted to do more than breathe in and out. He wanted to live.

CHAPTER EIGHT

LILA sat in front of her computer, aware she was only going through the motions of writing. What she was *really* doing was waiting for the phone to ring.

After being stranded on a mountain in the wilderness overnight—easily the biggest adventure of her life—it would be understandable if she took the afternoon off, even with the deadline looming.

But rather than being exhausted, Lila found she'd been wired when she got down off the mountain. She'd been practically buzzing with enthusiasm and joy. She had burst into her house, and thought she would put all this energy to good use.

She now knew *exactly* where to start her book on having the perfect Christmas. Chapter One: Christmas Fun in the Snow!

There was so much material: making snow angels, and even though the snow had not been sticky enough for building things, she could talk about snowmen and snow forts and snow carvings. Why not snow carvings for the front yard at Christmas time?

Then there was riding snowmobiles, which had been an exhilarating experience, one she wished everyone could have, the powerful machine cutting ribbons through un-tracked snow, the chance to see areas of pristine wilderness that no one else would ever see.

Then there were other outdoor cold weather activities that she had not yet tried, but couldn't wait to experience firsthand: tobogganing, skiing, skating, snowboarding, snowshoeing, ice fishing. The list was endless.

But with all that material, her computer screen remained completely, infuriatingly blank. *Start with what it feels like to go down that hill,* she ordered herself. If she could capture the thrill of careening down a snow-covered hill on a sled, she would have a runaway bestseller on her hands. She knew it.

She was not sure she had ever had as much fun in her entire life as riding that sled down that hill, her arms wrapped around Brody Taggert. It was wild and exhilarat-ing, and that was before the tumbles.

She had a sudden flash: the solid weight of his body on top of her, the look in his eyes, the heat of his lips melting snow off the hollow of her throat.

"A little too hot for a Christmas book," she muttered.

She began to wonder how much of the thrill had been because of the snow and the speed and the wind in her face, and how much had been because she had been with him.

And then doubt raced in. How could you start a book about having the perfect Christmas with a chapter on snow activities when anybody who had ever been around snow would know no instructions were required? Snow, plus spontaneity equaled more fun than a day at the amusement park. Way more fun.

Besides, wasn't it possible quite a bit of her audience would not have access to snow? She went to a map site, looked at a map of America and sighed. It would seem a large percentage of people in the U.S. did not live in places where there was snow. Other places would experience it so rarely that she could hardly make it a component in planning their perfect Christmas.

I'm never going to get this book done. Never.

Lila's eyes went to the clock on her screen. It was nearly four o'clock. Would Brody be down off the mountain yet? Was he thinking of her? If he was, did his heart do a funny flip-flop?

She surrendered to what she really wanted to do. She got up, went to her bedroom closet and tried to decide what she would wear to grab a bite to eat or *something* in Snow Mountain. With Brody Taggert.

How could she write about creating the perfect Christmas when Christmas suddenly didn't seem to matter to her at all? When she had become like a giddy teenage girl waiting for that special boy to phone, the one she had had a secret crush on all year, who had suddenly noticed she was alive?

"Lila," she implored herself. "Grow up. Be mature."

But she really didn't feel like being mature. Would mature people have given themselves over with such wild abandon to making snow angels? To recklessly riding that sled down the side of that mountain, whooping with joy and laughter?

No, she didn't want to be mature. It implied a certain stodginess, an addiction to safety and security that might make life predictable, but that could also make people dull and humorless and no fun at all to be around.

Even though Lila had changed her whole life—picked up and moved across the country, opened a new business—it hadn't really been an adventure because she had not changed herself. Or risked herself. It had all been outer stuff.

She wanted to be alive. And unafraid.

What would someone alive and unafraid wear out for a bite to eat with a man like Brody? She scanned her wardrobe, chose casual jeans, but a bold red silk shirt. She could make it daring—an outfit worthy of one who was unafraid—by leaving that top button undone. By wearing her black bra with it, the one that actually gave the illusion that she possessed cleavage.

She had turned to dig that bra, rarely worn, out of the back of her drawer, and it was then that the truth hit her like an avalanche. It hit her so squarely and so hard that she reeled back from her dresser, dropped her favorite silk blouse on the floor and sank onto the edge of her bed.

She understood why she had not been able to start her book, had not made one inch of headway into an instruction manual on creating the perfect Christmas.

Because she had fully intended to write a book based on trappings and trinkets, decorating, trees and activities. Like her move across the country, her book about Christmas had focused on all the outer stuff.

She'd missed the truth that was as old as Christmas itself. She had missed the very soul of what she was trying to write about. Christmas was about love.

It wasn't about the elves in Bandstand Park, it wasn't about finding the perfect tree, it wasn't about all that *stuff* she had filled her store with. She could see so clearly she had been trying to escape from the emptiness in her life by filling it with things and activities, accomplishments and accolades.

The emptiness had been there ever since fear had left her guarded, unwilling to risk anything that really mattered.

Shocked, Lila realized she had been trying desperately to create the illusion of Christmas without touching the heart of Christmas at all.

Lila suddenly felt as if she couldn't breathe as she slowly recognized what had come knocking on her door.

Love. An opportunity to love. To live more richly, to feel more deeply, to reconnect with a spirit she had lost.

She was falling in love with Brody Taggert.

And if she was courageous enough to embrace what she had been brought, she would experience gifts such as she had never known.

The phone rang.

With her heart beating hard with equal amounts of fear and exhilaration, Lila ran to pick it up.

Brody thought it had probably been a mistake to take Lila to the Sunday night smorgasbord at Chan's. Not because the food was not good, because it was. He was willing to place money that the almond chicken here was the best in the state. And Mama Chan had a special place in her heart for him. Whenever she saw him come in—even if it was smorg night—she hustled back to the kitchen and made him something special.

Tonight she set it down with flourish. "Fire bowl," she announced. "Szechuan-style prawn. Lover's special."

Which was exactly why it was a mistake to have brought Lila here. Because it was the only decent restaurant open Sunday night, and the whole town was here.

Unless he was mistaken, it would be going out over the wires before they had finished eating. He and Lila would be an item by tomorrow.

"Lover's special?" Lila whispered leaning toward him,

wide-eyed with mirth. Her hair was loose, catching the light, touching the slender place where her neck joined her shoulders.

She was wearing a red shirt that clung to her, and when she leaned forward like that he saw a place he wished he would have dribbled a little snow on when he had the chance.

"You won't think it's so funny when your aunt hears we were here."

"She'll hear?"

"Before you get home," he said dryly. "Half the town will be driving down your block tonight to see if my truck's parked there."

And tomorrow he'd be interrogated by her uncle, and be taking elbow shots at his ribs all day from the other guys; lots of winks, too.

"No!"

"Welcome to small-town life." He lifted his drink and toasted her with it.

"I feel pressured now," she said, and plucked one of the prawns out of the fire bowl with a chopstick. He, of course, had requested utensils.

"How do you get to know a person with the whole town watching?" she asked, her voice hushed.

"We could play with them," he suggested wickedly. "Give them something to talk about."

She got it right away. She leaned toward him even more. He felt a little bead of sweat break out on his brow. That bra was black.

She held out a prawn to him right on the end of her chopstick.

He could practically hear a pin drop in that restaurant

when he leaned forward, and nipped the prawn off the end of her chopstick with his teeth.

Only the funny thing was, when he looked in her eyes, dancing with merriment, and felt the warmth of her smile, it didn't feel as if they were pretending. It didn't feel as if they were giving the whole town something to talk about.

It felt exactly the way it had felt in that cabin, as if the world just contained the two of them, nothing else.

And that world smelled not of spicy Szechuan fire bowl prawns, but of wild strawberries.

He was brought back to the real world when Mr. And Mrs. Anderson stopped by, congratulated Lila on her work on Bandstand Park. They promised to be at the opening on the fifteenth of December, which Brody realized was only a few days away.

"Will you be at the opening?" she asked. And then with endearing shyness, "I'd like for you to come."

"Are there going to be cameras there?"

"Most likely."

"Good story," he said dryly. "I already wrote the ending for it, only they didn't capture it on camera that time. I don't want the fact I'm dating you to be some great feel-good story for the whole world."

"Are you dating me?" she asked, putting one of the prawns into her own mouth, which was at least as sexy as her feeding one to him.

"That's what *they* think," he hedged, nodding toward the other customers, most of whom were barely able to conceal their interest in the new couple, and many who weren't even trying.

"I don't care what they think. I want to know what you think. Is this our first date?"

The problem seemed to be that around her at least, he didn't think clearly at all. Because it was a first date? A first date implied a beginning. A desire to get to know each other. A possibility it was going to go to a second date, and further.

Further, where? he asked himself, and he thought of children laughing in the hayloft, and the way it had felt to spend the morning with her as if he was a young man, carefree, full of laughter and energy. And hope.

"Yeah," he said gruffly, "I guess it is. A first date."

"It doesn't feel like a first date," she said.

"That probably has something to do with sharing a bed together with a smelly dog," he said, his voice very low, the tables suddenly seeming way too close together in here.

"Whatever it is, I'm glad. I don't feel awkward. I just feel—"

He waited, aware he was holding his breath.

"Happy," she decided.

Happy. He could analyze that and decide it was way too much pressure to make another person happy. But that was the man he'd been yesterday. Today, he had hope.

"Yeah," he said. "Me, too." And then he stabbed a prawn with his unused chopstick and held it out to her. Laughing, she took it.

They fed each other every single prawn in that big bowl.

"You didn't tell me if you were coming to the grand reopening of Santa's Workshop at Snow Mountain," she said when they were done. He was aware he'd never been so sorry to empty a bowl of prawns.

"It really means a lot to you?"

"Really."

"Okay. Call it a second date. But I'm warning you, I'm bringing a gun."

"Very *unjolly* of you," she said disapprovingly.

"It shoots marshmallows. I'm going to aim it right at Jade Flynn if she comes anywhere near me."

They looked across each other over the empty dishes.

"Want to feed the rumor mill?" she asked him finally. "I have a video at my place. A Christmas movie. It's supposed to be hilarious."

He contemplated how her choice was telling him what kind of girl she was. And he realized he wanted to be exactly the kind of guy who could go watch a movie like that, and hold her hand, and laugh and go slow. Kiss her good-night on her porch when the movie was over.

"I don't like Christmas movies," he said and watched her pop open her fortune cookie.

She read it out loud. "You will travel to places you have never been," she said, and then smiled. "I think I already have. Read yours."

"Much joy in soup."

"It doesn't say that."

He passed it to her.

She read it. "It does say that." And then she broke up laughing, and so did he, and he could not remember a day in a long, long time where he had laughed so much. It felt so good.

"I have other movies," she said.

There was that *thing* again: *emotion* ruling him, wanting whatever it was he saw in her eyes.

"Okay," he said gruffly. "Let's go to your place and watch a movie."

In her house, her TV was hidden in a big cabinet on the end of the wall. He sorted through her DVD collection while she went and put on a pot of coffee. He snatched a recent action movie from the pile, noticed it was unopened.

He tore off the wrapper and set up the DVD player, then he wandered around, sniffing her candles to see if any of them smelled like strawberries. They didn't and he found himself at her tree. She'd brought it in too early and it was dropping needles all over the floor. He had never seen decorations like the ones on it. It was hung with perhaps a hundred little red and green velvet stockings, fur trimmed, each holding a tiny plush puppy. Only the puppies weren't cute.

"They're called Ugly Puppies," she said from behind him. "I just love them. There's one there that looks like Boo."

There was, too. He touched it, smiled. All that she was, and she loved ugly dogs, too. He'd better be careful or he was going to think she was the ideal woman. Or maybe he already did.

He turned to her.

"Is something wrong?" she said, and came and touched his face. "Brody, what is it?"

"Nothing. Put the movie on."

"What did you pick?"

He showed her the action movie DVD.

She shuddered a little. "I don't feel like watching it anymore. Let's talk."

"The most dreaded words a man can ever hear," he said wryly, but took a place on the couch. She sat right beside him, so close her knee was touching his. She poured coffee, took a sip, set her cup down and regarded him intently.

"Why do you hate Christmas so much, Brody?"

"I told you. I get to see the ugly underbelly of the season."

"So does my uncle Paul. He loves Christmas."

Brody sighed and closed his eyes. He wanted to tell her. Suddenly if felt like a burden he could not carry alone for one more second.

"My brother died," he said slowly. "This will be my seventh Christmas without him. It's not the same anymore. It's never going to be the same again. I don't feel any joy at Christmas. None. Only the space where he used to be."

It did feel good to say that because he wanted her to know the entire truth about him, before this thing went any further.

"That's what you should know about me," he said gruffly, "There's a hole in me so large nothing can fill it. I think maybe that hole is where my heart is supposed to be."

Lila's hand covered his, warm, surprisingly strong for such a small woman.

"Tell me about him," she said, and somehow it didn't feel like a request, but an order. Something she knew he had to do, something she knew she had to hear.

"Maybe some other time."

She was silent, and then she said softly, "Is this the brother you mentioned once before? You said his name was Ethan."

"Yeah, Ethan." Even saying his brother's name to her did not feel the way he had thought it would. It felt not as if he was sharing his sadness with her, but as if he was sharing something sacred with her. His memories of Ethan suddenly felt like water pushing behind a dam—it felt as if something would break if he did not let the pressure off, did not let something out.

She was silent, watching him, and he remembered how it had felt when he had told her about the Murphy girl.

As if the burdens he carried were lighter.

He closed his eyes, and told himself to shut up, but he

didn't. The scent of wild strawberries was so strong around him. If he just said one thing, let a little out, maybe the pressure he felt would fade.

"I was older than him. Three years. It seems like nothing now, but growing up I was the big brother. I was the leader, the instigator, the protector, the teacher."

Her hand tightened on his. "You feel guilty that he died," she guessed softly.

"Oh, yeah."

"Don't you think you might feel better if you told me?"

Brody opened his eyes and looked into the startling compassion of hers. He saw things there: wisdom and depth. He saw he could trust her, and he knew that being able to trust someone in a hard world was a rare and amazing gift, one he was not strong enough to throw back at her.

He saw that maybe, just maybe, she could move him toward the place he had never been able to arrive at: forgiveness of himself.

"We were really close," he said, closing his eyes again, remembering. "But really different. Ethan was quiet and thoughtful, artistic. I liked action movies or comedy, he liked drama and foreign language films. I liked playing hockey in the street, he'd rather read a book under a tree. If we went into the mountains together, I brought a rifle and bullets, he brought a sketchpad and charcoals.

"I was never afraid of anything—reckless, even. He was more cautious. Not timid, but he thought things through. He was always aware of consequences, I never gave them a thought.

"At the funeral I knew people were thinking that. They couldn't believe which brother had died.

"We didn't even look the same. I was dark, big, brawny,

a born football player, he was fair and kind of scrawny, like a long-distance runner.

"But given how different we were, we always got along. Always." He paused, knowing this was the turning point, the place where he gave himself over to what he saw in Lila's eyes or ran away from it.

The decision not to run filled him with the oddest warmth. "Until Darla," he admitted. This was the part of the tragedy he kept a secret within himself, that he had shared with no one, carrying the burden of his guilt and his shame alone.

"Tell me about that." She said it with a certain fierceness, as if she could see his soul, as if she knew intuitively this was the part that he needed to unload.

He swore under his breath, fighting with himself, wanting to get up and go home, *needing* something else entirely. Needing to be free of it.

"Tell me," she repeated.

He felt the surrender happen within himself, a sudden relaxing of tension that he had carried for more than six years.

"I was twenty that summer, working as a logger, full of myself. Making good money, strong as an ox. I started dating this girl named Darla. Honestly, looking back, I don't know what the attraction was. I think she asked for—and got—breast implants when she graduated from high school. She was the town 'It' girl. Blond, gorgeous, empty-headed. Probably my type, at that time, exactly."

The strangest thing was happening: Brody Taggert had always thought surrender would feel like an unbearable weakness. Instead, as he spoke, he felt stronger, as if he had been pinned under an enormous rock, under water, and now the weight was being lifted.

"Darla," he said, "was not Ethan's type at all. But he fell hard for her. From the first time I brought her home to have a hamburger before we went to the drive-in, he was smitten. After a few weeks, he started acting like he had something to prove—shoving me, tackling me from behind, yelling at me, calling me names."

With every word he spoke, damning as they were, Brody could feel himself rising up through murkiness, struggling toward light.

"That must have been hard for you. To go from being his hero, to *that*."

"I don't know. The summer of my colossal self-centeredness. I was irritated by it. Annoyed.

"In retrospect, I can see Ethan was really, really mad. As if he'd figured out guys like me were going to get girls like that, and guys like him weren't.

"If he'd lived long enough he would have figured out that girls like that always turn out to be more headache than you could ever imagine, and that the kind of guys who went for them, like me, ended up yearning for those wholesome, smart kind of girls that you could actually enjoy being with. Though by then Mr. Macho has usually managed to burn most of his bridges, and a nice girl wouldn't give him the time of day."

Brody was silent, and had Lila said anything he probably wouldn't have gone on, but she was silent, her hand warm and still on his knee, and the sensation of rising toward the light, of being suddenly freed, increased.

"Things came to a head and Ethan and I had a fight. I mean not really a fight. He wanted to come with Darla and I to the swimming hole, I'm sure I had something in mind that I didn't want little brother around for. I'm sure I'd said no to him before, but that time he just started swinging at me. I was kind of trying to hold him off while he was throwing wilder and wilder punches, getting madder and madder because I was egging him on by laughing at him. We broke one of my mom's vases. She collected cranberry glass. That vase was from 1854 or something.

"Ethan was so upset. We hid the broken vase. We were like brothers again, not like combatants, trying to figure out what to do."

He actually smiled, remembering. "We figured wild strawberries. We went to that hunter's shack, the same one you and I were at, and spent the night, and the next morning we went looking.

"It was the way things used to be. Just me and him. A truce between us. We joked and talked. He was such a good guy. Deep. Connected to spirit. We stayed one more night, I think both of us were a bit scared to tell Mom about that vase, even with an offering of wild strawberries.

"Ethan drew some pictures that night by the lamplight. The next morning we brought Mom the meager offering of wild strawberries, and even though they were her favorite thing, she was madder than a wet hen about her vase.

"So we decided to clear out for the day. I hoped the truce would last, I *wanted* to be with him. The day before had been so great. So I invited him to come, after all, with Darla and I to the swimming hole above Snow Peak Falls."

He shuddered, fell silent.

"Tell me," she said, insistent, and suddenly it felt as if her voice, her eyes were the light he was struggling toward.

"It used to be my favorite place in the whole world. A pool of green water between two rock faces. Ethan and I used to jump off the rocks into the water.

"The pool was in a kind of back eddy, the river went by there pretty swiftly. That pool was the last tranquil water before rapids and then the falls.

"So, we were spending the day there. A perfect summer day. And then, in one split second, it all changed. Everything changed. Forever."

"What happened?" Lila whispered.

"A puppy was being washed down the fast part of the river, we could hear it whining and crying in pure terror, then we could see its head bobbing in and out of the water. Darla started having hysterics.

"And this is the part no one knows except me: I remember my brother looking at her, and then at me, and this look came over his face, like finally, he was going to show her who was the better man. By the time I made a grab for him, he was already gone. He leaped into the rapids after that puppy, and was swept away before I had even registered completely what had happened."

"Brody," she whispered, and the fact that his pain had become her pain was the thing that finally made his head break water, finally allowed him to feel as though he could breathe again. He was not alone. Not anymore.

"Ethan didn't have the physical strength to hold out in that water. Once it hits the rapids, it's boiling. You can actually hear the water picking up boulders, they rumble around under the surface. Hell, I don't think I had that kind of strength.

"But the difference was, I knew it. I knew it couldn't be done. The puppy was doomed. That was another difference between us. He was a born optimist. I was a born realist."

He stopped, took a deep breath. Even the air tasted different: pure.

"A search team found him the next day," Brody said, quietly. "They said he probably died instantly, his head hit a rock. He didn't suffer. I guess suffering is for the living."

"You've suffered ever since, haven't you?" she asked softly.

"Nobody it touched was ever the same. All my mom could think of was that she'd been mad at him. Our family started to disintegrate. I couldn't stop asking all these questions. Why hadn't I gone after the dog? I was the bigger one, the stronger one. Maybe I could have pulled it off. Why hadn't I been able to grab my brother before he did something so stupid, and for such a dumb reason?

"Ethan, my cautious brother, died trying to win a girl. My girl. I went on self-destruct. Your uncle pulled me from my own rapids just before I went over the falls.

"Your uncle. And Boo."

"Boo?"

He felt his throat tighten. "Boo. The puppy survived. No one knows how. They found her right beside my brother's body, snuggled into him, nearly dead herself. But she had enough life in her that she growled and tried to bite the guy who tried to take her away from Ethan. She was in a bad way, her legs were broken, that's why they never grew properly.

"People didn't understand why I took her. Hell, I didn't really understand it myself. But I did take her, and she *needed* things from me. She needed me to feed her, and hold her, and take her outside. I had to learn to be responsible, and to put her needs ahead of my own. That was a lifeline, that I had to think of one little thing besides myself and my hurt and my anger.

"One day, I had set a beer mug on the floor—I was drinking hard back then—and she got her head stuck inside it. And I heard myself laughing. When I thought I would never laugh again, I heard myself laughing.

"Pathetic as it might seem, that dog gave me something to live for. In a way, she forced me to be a man my brother might have been proud of."

He stopped the story short. He stopped it short of the words that would totally threaten his control, that could take away every gain sharing his tragedy with Lila had given him.

I might lose Boo now, too, and I don't know what I'll do when that link to my brother is gone.

No, he wasn't going to lose her. Look at how Boo had been the last few days, so happy, so full of energy, eating with such appetite.

He looked at Lila for the first time since he had started talking. She was crying, great, huge tears slithering down her cheeks.

He felt something clawing at his own throat, something smarting behind his eyes.

Her arms went around him, and she pulled his head onto her breast and stroked his hair, her voice a healing balm that melted over him.

Like Lila, Brody realized he had not felt safe for a long, long time. He walked in the awareness that a good life could turn bad in a blink.

But in her arms he was aware that the opposite was also true: that a sad life could become happy again. That a man could feel safe even in an unpredictable world.

With her arms around him, with her whispering words in his ear, with the delight of the day at the cabin so fresh in his mind, he became aware that he was very close to be-lieving in a miracle.

And that miracle had a name. It's name was love.

But right now he was exhausted and drained, and though he wanted to stay, he knew where it would go, and he knew he didn't want it to go there as a reaction.

When he made love to Lila, it was going to be because they had both made a conscious decision that was right for them. It wasn't going to be an impulse.

Still, he left her reluctantly.

When he got into his own house, for the first time in six and a half years, he was greeted with total silence.

"Boo," he called.

But she did not come. No careening around the kitchen corner, tail wagging, tongue hanging, eyes adoring on his face.

And he knew right then, in this brand-new emptiness, that she was gone. He had dared to hope, he had gambled on a miracle and he had lost.

Brody Taggert went down on his knees, and felt the break of his heart.

It broke for all his losses.

And for the loss of that thing he had grabbed on to so briefly: hope, a sense of the miraculous.

So, there were no miracles after all. He did not want to love again. Or hope again. Or believe again. Not ever.

Those things could bring a powerful man to his knees. Those things could make a powerful man realize he had no real power at all.

Asking a man like him to hope, to believe, to love, was like asking a warrior to face the world without his weapons. To trust there was a place safe enough for a man to be unarmed.

And life was reminding him there wasn't. There was no place that safe. Not even the sanctuary he thought he had glimpsed, briefly and beautifully, in Lila's arms.

CHAPTER NINE

BRODY stood before his boss in Hutch's office. He'd been summoned at the end of his shift, and he was pretty sure there'd been a complaint, maybe more than one. He felt ice-cold inside, not mean, but indifferent to people whining about getting tickets so close to Christmas.

Somehow they wanted *him* to be responsible for the fact they were piling Christmas gifts so high they couldn't see out the back windows of their vehicles, for the fact they were rushing here and there in frantic bursts of pre-Christmas activity.

"If you don't want a ticket," he'd told Herb Waters, "try not speeding through the school zone."

Herb hadn't liked that.

But if Herb had complained, Hutch said nothing about it.

"Karl Jamison wants to retire," Hutch said. "He said he's getting married."

That penetrated the icy wall around Brody slightly. "Jamison is getting married? Who would marry him?"

"Apparently, Jeanie Harper would."

For a moment, Brody hurt. Jamison, rough-spoken, tough as nails, was willing to give love a chance? Jamison was willing to do what it took not to be lonely anymore? For a moment he wished it was him.

But only for a moment, and then he shrugged off that thought by thinking of that fresh mound of dirt in his backyard, Boo wrapped in her favorite blanket with her favorite toy, a neon-orange Frisbee, in the bottom of that cold, cold hole.

"And like everything Karl wants to do, he wants to do it yesterday. He told me by the end of February he's going to be on his honeymoon cruise on the Caribbean."

The warmth of being with somebody you loved in the tropics tried to touch him, but again Brody shrugged, physically, told himself he *loved* the cold and had no wish to escape it. Hutch seemed to be expecting a comment, but Brody said nothing.

"You got any ideas about who could replace him?"

The icy shield came down just a bit. He knew a guy who needed a chance, a lifeline, just as he had once needed one. "Mike Stevens would probably be a good bet," Brody said.

Hutch grinned at him. "Funny you should say that. That's exactly who I had in mind." He noticed Brody wasn't smiling back, and his brow furrowed.

"The phone's been ringing off the hook all day. I'm being accused of having the world's biggest Scrooge on the department. And not Karl, either."

Brody said nothing.

"What's wrong, son?" Hutch asked him, his voice uncharacteristically gentle.

Please don't call me that. I'm just barely holding it together as it is.

Sooner or later someone was going to notice the dog wasn't tagging along at his heel, shedding hairs all over the backseat of the police cruiser. Sooner or later he was going to have to say it.

It might as well be sooner. "Boo died," Brody said grimly.

Hutch's mouth dropped open. "No," he said, and then gruffly, "How?"

"She had cancer."

"Aw, hell, Brody." The chief's eyes were tearing over.

Brody steeled himself. A voice that was not his own, cold and hard, said, "She was just a dog."

Hutch looked angry. "She sure as hell wasn't just a dog. She was one of us. Maybe we never officially made her a K-9, because they probably would have made her go to police dog school or some damn fool thing for insurance purposes, but Brody, that dog was one of us."

That pesky warmth was trying to penetrate the ice again. Brody did not trust himself to speak.

"Brody you know, probably better than most, that life gives us hard things to deal with. Really hard. But what I want you to know is that you're always given what you need to deal with those things. Always. But you got to look, son. You got to have a heart open enough to recognize them when they come."

It was a rare piece of philosophy from Hutch. Brody knew what his boss was saying was true. Boo had come along right when he needed her most.

And now an angel waited to help him through this. If his heart was open. But he was not sure it was. Or could be. Or ever would be again.

When the lifeline was tossed to him this time, he was not sure he would grab it. Because the price of grabbing it was opening up a heart that felt just fine frozen solid, where nothing could touch it and nothing could hurt.

"You let me know if there's anything I can do, Brody."

"I will," Brody said, but he knew he wouldn't.

"And now, ladies and gentleman, Snow Mountain welcomes you to A Celebration of the Season."

Lila watched as the ladies from the Baptist Church choir filed into the darkened park and up the stairs of the freshly painted bandstand. They wore their new long red robes, and the only light in the park came from the candles they held. The crowds, people all the way from Spokane and Coeur d'Alene, were three deep against the white picket fence that surrounded the park.

She scanned the expectant audience. Still no Brody. She hadn't talked to him since that night at her place when he had told her about his brother, but he had said he would be here, and one thing about Brody Taggert was that he was a man you could count on.

She shivered just thinking of him, of the way she felt when he looked at her, of the way she felt when his lips were on the hollow of her throat.

The ladies opened with "O Christmas Tree," and as they sang, the tree that Lila and Brody had harvested blinked on blue light after blue light, until finally the star at the very top winked on, shining brilliantly.

They sang "Deck the Halls," and the rest of the lights in the trees and on the fences, around the bandstand itself, lit all at once, colorful beacons of cheer. The crowd broke into applause.

Next came "Rudolph the Red-Nosed Reindeer," and spotlights shone on each reindeer in turn: this one rearing, that one kicking up his heels, one moving his head, another nudging a sleigh, one pawing the ground impatiently.

Where was Brody? Even he, as cynical as he pretended to be about this, would have to be impressed with this wonderful choreography of sound and light.

As the choir sang "Santa Claus is Coming to Town" all the elves lit up and began to move: this one wrapping a present, that one hammering a toy, this one filling boxes, that one picking his nose. The crowd howled with laughter, and the elf's eyes widened at them and then he smiled bashfully.

And then the park was plunged into darkness again, and only candles lit it. A solo voice began to sing "Silent Night," and then the crowd was joining in singing, too, the park and the street reverberating with the special miracle of that song.

When it was done, the lights came back on all at once to the thunderous applause of the audience. The choir left the bandstand stage, and it was empty save for a huge throne.

And then a child's high-pitched voice. "But where is Santa?"

It couldn't have been more perfect if there had been a script, which there wasn't. A hush went over the crowd. And then from behind the bandstand, waving and carrying a sack of toys, came a real live Santa.

Even though Brody had claimed there was no such thing, surely if there was it would look exactly like Karl Jamison did in this moment.

Brody was going to regret missing this for the rest of his life, Lila thought, casting another glance around for him. Even in this crowd she knew he would stand out. But he simply wasn't there.

"Hello, children," Karl roared. "Ho, ho, ho."

He was so fierce in his greeting that a child in the front row whimpered. But the older children were not the least intimidated, and yelled with excitement.

Jamison took his place on the throne in the middle of the bandstand and Jeanie Harper opened the gate to the red carpeted sidewalk that led right to his lap. Children, giddy with excitement, surged forward and lined up for their chance to tell Santa all their secrets and dreams, and wishes and hopes.

"Lila Grainger," Jade Flynn said to her, "you must be very proud of your town tonight."

Lila fixed a smile on her face as the TV lights were turned on her, but she was aware she did not feel like smiling.

Where was Brody? He had said he would be here. Maybe not quite promised, but she had always taken him completely as a man who could be counted on to do exactly as he said every single time.

Maybe Brody was watching from somewhere, waiting for the TV crew to disappear.

Lila forced herself to focus on Jade, talked about the community spirit that had come together for the park.

She concluded, "And I need to give special thanks to the Snow Mountain Police Department who provided us with Santa, and especially to Officer Brody Taggert for finding that beautiful Christmas tree. I also want to thank Town Council and all the people who sent donations and cards and letters so that Snow Mountain did not have to cancel Christmas."

Maybe that would stop Brody from getting the hate mail, not that, at this precise moment, Lila felt he deserved her intervention. And not that he had ever appreciated it in the past.

Jade asked her a few more questions, then wrapped it up. It was wrong to be disappointed that a marshmallow bullet had not zoomed in out of the darkness and knocked that silly red angora beret right off Jade's head.

But as the TV van pulled away there was still no sign of Brody. Lila went over to the hot chocolate stand and took her turn dispensing hot drinks to the crowd, reminding them Snow Mountain's stores would be open late tonight for their Christmas shopping convenience.

It seemed like hours later that the last child had sat on Santa's knee, the crowds around the park had dispersed to the downtown area.

Still, no Brody.

Lila decided to wait there just a little longer. She sat on a bench, pulled her coat tight around herself and tried to enjoy the light display, the antics of the repaired elves and reindeer. Later tonight, the city crew would bring the mechanized Santa in, and put him on that throne where Jamison had sat.

Something moved in the darkness, and she turned to look, her heart beating with hope. But it was her aunt who came and sat beside her.

"It's beautiful, Lila, better than ever. I missed it all more than I thought. Main Street just didn't seem right without it. Neither did Snow Mountain."

"Thanks." She hesitated and then said, "Do you know if Brody got called in to work unexpectedly?"

It became obvious her aunt was holding back tears.

"Is he okay?" she asked, stunned by the panic she felt, as if her world would never be the same if Brody Taggert was not in it.

Marla blinked back tears. "Boo died, Lila."

"Boo?" She felt the shock of it in the pit of her stomach. A fist closed around her heart. "Oh, no," she whispered. "What happened?"

"Brody told Paul she had cancer."

Lila felt the shock of that, too. Why hadn't Brody said something?

"Is Brody okay?" she asked.

Marla looked sad. "Probably not."

Lila got up off the bench. "I need to be with him. He needs someone to be with him."

Her aunt stayed her with a touch on Lila's arm. "Maybe you should give him some time, Lila. I don't think he wants to be with anyone right now. He won't want sympathy. He hates it."

Her aunt had been there when Brody had dealt with another tragedy. She would probably know. But still, in her heart, Lila thought, broken, *even me?* But if he had wanted her to go to him, wouldn't he have called her? Wouldn't he have told her Boo was ill?

A first date did not exactly mean their stars were joined.

But the things he had shared with her had made it feel as if he had trusted her, as if he knew his heart would be safe with her. If that was true, why hadn't he called?

Still, she took a miss on visiting the stores that were still open and went straight home to call him. His answering machine picked up after the second ring.

"Tag. Leave a message."

"Brody, it's Lila. I just heard about Boo. I'm so sorry. I didn't know her very long, but—" her voice cracked "—long enough to love her. Please call me."

But he didn't, and somehow even with Bandstand Park lit up so bright that its glow could be seen from a satellite, it felt as if her Christmas was going to be wrapped in darkness.

It was too soon to love him; rationally she knew that and accepted that. Their relationship had not deepened to a point where he wanted to share his sorrow with her, where he would invite her into his weakest moments, when he would surrender to leaning on her.

But even though she knew that rationally, her heart would not accept it as true. Her heart ached for him, and for his loneliness. Her heart waited for him to call, to invite her back into his world.

Her book on creating a perfect Christmas was now officially on hold. She couldn't give away something she did not have, and she did not have a joyous spirit.

It was two days before Christmas. Brody was alone, and he told himself that was exactly what he wanted and deserved.

He'd listened to Lila's message at least a dozen times, finding solace in her voice, *wanting* to call her, and yet not wanting her to see him like this.

Broken up over a dog, for God's sake. It had been over a week, and he was not mending, not healing, not moving on. Maybe *frozen* was the safest way to be, but it wasn't what he wanted to give Lila. He wasn't sure he had what he wanted to give her, and what she deserved.

What she deserved was a man with the ability to trust in life, a warrior who could protect her and be strong, yes, but who had the ability to put away the armor.

His house suddenly depressed him, even with the great television set. He hated the television offerings this close to Christmas, and he hated days with no football or hockey games scheduled.

After flipping through his three hundred channel options several thousand times, he finally threw down the channel changer in disgust. After a while, he went into the basement and pulled out a box.

Not quite sure what had drawn him here, he opened it.

Ethan's sketches. One by one, he went through them. Why not? He was depressed anyway.

But as he looked through the sketches, his depression did not deepen, it lessened. The ice seemed to fall a bit more from his heart with each sketch he looked at.

Somehow Ethan had captured not just the essence of their childhood—swimming holes and tire swings, the old barn at dusk, laundry on the line, two boys sitting on a rickety wharf, bare feet and fishing poles in the water— but the essence of *them*.

Carefree days, that had been so pure, so filled with the careless love that one brother had for another, so filled with their bond, a bond Brody had not fully recognized until it had been broken.

And then, nearing the bottom of the box, Brody found a drawing his brother had done of Darla. He started to go right by it, with no more than a glance, just as he went right by her with no more than a glance every time she drove by him with her vanload of kids.

But something stopped him, and he looked at the picture more carefully.

Just as his brother had captured the essence of brothers when he drew pictures of them both, so had he captured Darla's.

Brody had always seen Darla as his *ideal* girl at that time in his life—too much makeup and too little clothing, just as eager as him to get into the backseat of his car.

But Ethan had captured her looking off into the distance, something wistful and innocent in her face.

He suddenly realized he had completely misunderstood Ethan's anger at him that summer. Completely.

Ethan had seen who Darla really was, a girl, not quite

the woman she was determined to convince the world she was. In her eyes, in that sketch, were the dreams of the children she now hauled to hockey and soccer. Darla had wanted a life Brody had no intention of giving her and Ethan, with his uncanny ability to see people, had recognized that.

Ethan had seen his brother was completely unworthy of her. Ethan had known Brody would never see Darla the way he had shown her in this drawing. No, Brody had seen her only through his own self-serving lens: willing, eager to please in all the right ways, he had unabashedly *used* her. He had practically swaggered with his own arrogance that summer, so full of himself and testosterone and the self-centered restlessness of young men.

Unwillingly, Brody revisited those final moments on the river, and with this drawing in his hand, he saw it all differently. It was not that Ethan had been trying to *prove* who had been the better man.

Ethan *had* been the better man. He had seen Darla's innocence and wanted to protect it, and her, from the harsh reality of what was going to happen next if someone didn't do something. One quick glance at his brother had confirmed Brody sure as hell wasn't going to jump in that water for a measly little puppy.

Of course, in the end, Ethan had not accomplished what he wanted. Nowhere close. But there was pure *honor* in a man who would try to protect a young woman from a horrible experience, even if it put his own life at risk.

And it had taken that tragedy to humble Brody, to remove the arrogance from him, to take him to a place where he had realized slowly, and often painfully, the world was not there to serve him. He was there to serve the world.

Not that he was great at it. Or perfect. But at least today he was a man who could see the tragic beauty of a child who would steal a game for her brother.

Because he knew what it was to love a brother.

And at least today, he knew the value of a good dog.

At least today, he could look at someone like Lila Grainger, and *see* her.

But deserve her? He wasn't sure about that.

He set the drawing of Darla back in the box, gently, and took out the last two pieces of paper.

The last two drawings were spectacular.

One was a charcoal sketch of the hunter's cabin, and somehow, though Ethan showed only the building, you could hear the laughter coming from behind those walls, sense how many boys had become men in this place, sense how it had provided a place away, a place to be, a place to understand all that really mattered.

And the last drawing in the box was a wild strawberry plant, the only one of Ethan's drawings Brody had ever seen colored.

The strawberry hung beneath the broad, serrated edges of the plant's leaves, so bright red and shiny Brody could almost taste it. And he could certainly smell it.

He looked again at the picture of the cabin, thought of all the wood he had left there and the credo Ethan had lived by.

He put the rest of the pictures back in the box, but kept those last two out. He would have the strawberry picture framed to give to his mother when he flew down to see her and his dad in January.

In the emptiness of his house, he said out loud, "You left more than you took."

He didn't know if he was talking to Ethan or Boo or

maybe to both of them. He only knew that even though he was absolutely alone he didn't feel alone at all.

He felt as if he had been heard.

And he felt as if, finally, it was his turn. To leave more than he took. He only had one day left, and a lot to do, especially since he would be battling all those other self-centered guys who treated Christmas as if it was an inconvenience, who left all the things they had to do until the last minute.

Still, even with that, Brody was aware of feeling the first little tickle of happiness he had felt since Boo had gone. The first sense that maybe, just maybe, he was going to be all right after all.

Christmas Eve. The worst one of her life, Lila decided morosely. Oh, the store had done exceedingly well, and her Internet business had increased sales over last year by fifty-three percent.

People were coming in all the time to thank her for saving Christmas in Snow Mountain, and she was still answering mail generated by the news story Jade Flynn had done of the opening of Santa's Workshop at Bandstand Park.

But the book, *How to Have a Perfect Christmas,* was a complete loss. She had missed her deadline, and she did not really see the point in asking for more time.

She really had nothing to say on the topic of how to have a perfect Christmas.

Because really, hers *looked* perfect. Her house decorated beautifully, her business a success, the Santa's Workshop display not only saved, but attracting traffic and visitors to Snow Mountain from all over Washington and Idaho.

But her Christmas just didn't *feel* right.

She longed for Brody. She longed to crash through his silence, his rejection of her caring, and be there for him anyway, whether he liked it or not. Unfortunately she knew better than anyone what that felt like. She knew what it felt like to be the object of unwanted attention and affection. She could not chase Brody like some crazed stalker, ignore the boundaries he had set as if she knew better than he did what was good for him.

Just as Christmas was about what you could give, about the spirit rather than the trinkets and lights and presents, so was love.

It wasn't all about hearts beating fast, and heated looks, what to wear. It wasn't all about those fireworks elements that were so breathtaking. It wasn't like a storybook where everything just unfolded perfectly and everyone lived happily ever after.

Love was asking her to go deeper, to dig deeper within herself. Love was asking her to respect him, not to meet her own needs through him, but to trust that he knew what was best for himself.

"Though he obviously doesn't," she said out loud.

Brody wasn't going to come to her. It was not his nature.

She stood before her glorious tree, and felt her eyes mist over. "I want him to be happy," she whispered. "I wish him happiness even if that means he doesn't choose me."

There it was. The spirit of Christmas, and indeed the spirit of love.

Not about trinkets and lights, not about stolen kisses and heated looks: about a selflessness of spirit.

She went to her tree and looked at the Ugly Puppy ornament that looked so much like Boo. She removed it from the tree, and slipped it into her sweater pocket.

She would give it to her uncle Paul to give to Brody, just so he knew she was thinking of him, she wished him well. She would put her prayer for his well-being and happiness into it, and then she would let go.

Touching that ornament in her pocket, worth under four dollars, it felt as if it would be the purest gift she had ever given. A gift that asked nothing in return, that only gave.

There was an unexpected knock at her front door, and she noticed, with a small smile, that she did not startle. And that she did not feel afraid. She went and opened the door without looking out the peephole first.

And blinked back tears at how swiftly she had been rewarded for her awkward attempt at selfless love.

Because he stood there, Brody, gazing at her with a look in his eyes that she could only have dreamed of.

The look of a man who had been away to wars, and had found his way home through the sheer bravery of his heart.

"Hi," she said softly, the woman who had waited, and known, and done her best to trust that he would know what his own heart needed.

She reached out and touched his cheek with her fingertips, tenderly, looked deep into his eyes. "I'm so sorry about Boo."

He did not flinch or try to back away from her touch. He said, his voice hoarse, "I know, Lila. Thank you."

"Are you coming in?"

"I was hoping you'd come out. I want to show you something."

He waited while she pulled on her boots and jacket, and then he took her to his truck.

He opened the door, pulled out a package, handed it to her. It was a tiny gift bag, silver, with a white bow on it. She peeked in and saw a bottle of *Effervescence,* the scent this year, unbelievably expensive in Lila's mind.

She felt a surge of disappointment. She couldn't even wear scent. Just as she was trying to think of a way to thank him for the gift she didn't want, that said he had not listened to her as completely as she had thought he had, that didn't express what she wanted their relationship to be *at all,* he spoke, unusually uncertain for Brody.

"I need your advice. The lady at the drugstore said that a young girl would love this. What do you think? For a fifteen-year-old?"

Just when she thought she had got it, when she had accepted love wasn't all about her, she got this reminder what love was really about after all.

"Would that be for a fifteen-year-old girl who took something that didn't belong to her? A little girl who really loves her brother?" she asked softly.

He ducked his head, looked wildly uncomfortable. "Yeah."

"It's perfect," Lila told him, handing him back the bag.

"Are you sure?" he asked, frowning.

"Positive." How could you love a person as much as she loved Brody Taggert in this moment without shattering into a million pieces of dazzling light?

"Oh, good. I just thought I'd get your opinion. I trust your opinion."

"What's that?" she asked as he put the small silver bag beside another parcel on his truck seat. The other parcel, clumsily wrapped, was the exact size and shape of a video game.

"Ah, nothing."

The tears began to gather in her eyes as she recognized *him.* Saw exactly who Brody Taggert was. It was not what he showed people, not even what he wanted people to believe about him, but it was who he was.

Just as she had known all along, from the first moment she had set eyes on him, the world was a better place because he was in it, whether he knew it or not. And he so obviously didn't.

"Tower of the Rebels?" she asked him softly.

He shifted uneasily from foot to foot, didn't answer.

"Can I come with you? To deliver them?" Softly, "Santa?"

He snorted. "I'm not Santa, and I'm not good company right now."

"I know that," she said. "You don't have to be. You don't have to say a single word to me, Brody Taggert. I already know who you are."

And suddenly Lila Grainger knew exactly how you had a perfect Christmas. You found someone who needed your love and your gifts, and you gave them.

You gave them with no expectation of return, with not one single thought about what was in it for you.

You gave your love just the way Brody had given those gifts. Letting the truth of the universe pass through you, taking no credit at all.

And that, she thought with a sigh, was how to have a perfect Christmas.

Brody Taggert wasn't sure he should have brought Lila here. Clements Street didn't exactly fit with her storybook fantasies of Christmas.

Close to downtown, the houses were old, but not the lovingly restored kind of old. The falling-down kind of old.

He stopped his truck in front of a house with more tar paper than shingle showing on the side. The porch was leaning. A sign, brass and classy, as if in defiance of the poorness of the house, hung at the end of the walkway. *The Murphys.*

He took the gifts and went up the walk, slid open the outer door quietly, set the packages inside and came back down the walk without ringing the doorbell.

"That was one of the nicest things I've ever seen a person do, Brody Taggert," she said when he got back in the truck.

"Probably just plain dumb," he said. "You can't begin to make a dent in the sadness at this time of year."

He put the truck in gear and drove away. Somehow, without really intending to, he ended up at Bandstand Park. He turned off the engine.

"It looks great," he said, and then admitted, "I missed it. The town didn't *feel* right without it. It makes me think maybe you can put a dent in the sadness, after all. Anybody can come here and bring their kids here. It's free. It feels happy."

"Next year we'll make it even better," she vowed. "We'll make the tree a Secret Santa tree. We'll put a tag on it for every child in this town who needs a gift."

"I have something for you," he said, amazed by how shy, how uncertain he suddenly felt. "It isn't much. And I'm no gift wrapper."

In fact he'd used up the one sheet of Christmas paper he'd been able to unearth on *Tower of the Rebels,* so he'd wrapped this in brown paper. With a touch that he thought at the time had been decorative, but now just looked plain stupid, he'd tied it with a piece of hemp twine.

He handed her his gift.

She opened it carefully, as if she was unwrapping china, no ripping and tearing for her.

Inside that package was a framed charcoal drawing of the cabin where she and Brody had spent the night.

"It's beautiful," she breathed. "I can't believe how accurately it's captured the soul of that little sanctuary deep in the wilderness."

She looked at the signature on the drawing.

"Ethan," she said quietly, and even though he knew she had just read the name as it was signed, it sounded oddly and beautifully like a greeting.

And he understood, suddenly, what he was doing. Inviting her into a life, a life that held a past and a present, held light and darkness, held joy and sorrow. He was inviting her into a life where he'd had to fight and fight hard to stay strong, into a life where he had just realized sometimes being strong meant laying down the weapons, taking off the armor.

Sometimes, what took the most strength of all was to be vulnerable to another human being. To stop fighting. To surrender.

To say to love, *you have wounded me, but I am prepared to be wounded again. For to live without you is to live in a place so lonely and so empty it makes life a living hell.*

The cab of his truck became so filled with the scent of wild strawberries that he thought he might weep.

She looked him full in the face, and he realized she did know who he was.

He saw in her eyes that she knew him. That he would never be able to hide one thing from her, not even his weakness, not even his sorrow. He knew that if he ever lost himself, he would just be able to look in her eyes and find who he was all over again.

Instead of the intensity of the love shining from her feeling frightening, it felt good, like a man who had been lost in a storm suddenly sighting lights, and following them, drawing closer and closer to the place he could rest, the place where he could be home.

With the scent of wild strawberries all around him, he got it.

He got what the chief had been trying to tell him.

Boo, with her uncanny sixth sense, had known from the first moment she had seen Lila and begun to hum happily.

His dog had recognized in that way that dogs do, that love was there, and that the one she was leaving behind would be okay as long as love was there.

His dog, who had been sent to him, when he wanted her least and needed her most.

Life *was* hard. Love *was* hard. It made no promises, it offered no guarantees, it dished up its fair share of sorrow.

What had Hutch said? A man was always given what he needed. Always.

Tag slid Lila a look, and his heart sighed.

She pressed something into his hand, and he looked down to see the Christmas ornament that had hung on her tree that looked like Boo. He blinked hard, then hung it on his mirror, Boo watching over them.

He got it. The scent of wild strawberries. He got it. His brother, somehow, someway, letting him know. *Go on. Live.*

Not that Brody believed in that kind of thing.

But if he ever was going to, it would be in the cab of his truck as church bells struck midnight to remind the world it could only truly be changed by one thing.

Love.

Everything else—power, money, success, possessions, life itself, everything else—would come and go.

But love would remain.

It would remain and forever change the hearts of the

people it had touched. His brother was gone, but the lessons his brother had taught him would remain, and would go on through him.

"You know," he said to Lila, softly looking out over the park, "at my brother's funeral the minister said all love leads to loss. And for the longest time I believed that was true.

"But now I see something different. You might lose the person, but not the gift they've given you."

He thought of Ethan, and all the years they had shared. He thought of Ethan's wonderful, generous spirit, his sense of honor, the way he saw the world, how he saw straight past people's trapping and right to their souls. And he understood. He had been living in those moments of death, rather than appreciating all that Ethan had been while he lived.

He was ready, now, to make the next step.

"Ethan would want me to live again. Fully. He'd especially want me to love again." And then added softly, "Fully."

Lila sighed beside him, and he knew she understood.

He embraced the gift that was being offered to him. The true gift, the only real gift of the season of miracles.

"Lila," he said, "come on over here, squish right up beside me."

She did, eagerly, as if she had been waiting all her life to show him who he really was.

He put his arm around her, kissed her, drank in her sweetness and the absolute truth about himself.

And then he put the truck in gear and drove toward a future that held the laughter of children in haylofts. It was a future that shone like a star worth following, if a man had the strength and the faith to believe in what he would find at the end of it.

He heard himself saying words he had thought he would never say again.

"Lila, I love you. Fully." His voice was hoarse with emotion, but somehow along the road of this incredible journey he had embarked on, he had realized emotion was not the enemy. Not at all. Saying those words filled him, to the top, and then, when she said them back, his sense of well-being brimmed over, a well of liquid gold within him.

EPILOGUE

"COLBY ETHAN TAGGERT," Lila called, "you come down from that hayloft right now."

Silence.

"I mean it."

Chubby little legs appeared at the trap door, and Lila held her breath as her three-year-old son's legs hung suspended for a moment, but then, mercifully, touched the top ladder rungs.

She had just turned her back on him for a blink while she tried to find the toboggan that they were going to need when Brody got home, and Colby loved that hayloft unreasonably. She often heard him chattering away up there to his imaginary buddy.

Colby came down that ladder like a little monkey, dropped at her feet, looked at her with wide-eyed innocence, as if she had not told him a thousand times not to go up there unsupervised.

Did he have to be so like his father? His dark hair was tousled and woven through with hay, his eyes, green and gold and brown, danced with enough warmth to melt a rock. Her son was fearless, charming, devil-may-care, irrepressible. And he was only three! What would he be like at fourteen?

"Kitties up there, Mommy."

"Really?"

"Come see," he pleaded. "Please?"

She looked at the ladder, rested a hand on the enormous belly that meant she wasn't going to be joining the guys for any sledding anytime soon, sighed and gave in. At the top of the ladder, puffing, she paused, and let her eyes adjust to the light. Sure enough, playing in the hay of the loft were three exuberant kittens, a black, an orange and a calico.

She forgot the toboggan totally, found a piece of string and she and Colby played with the kittens until the rafters rang with their laughter.

That's what Brody heard, as soon as he entered the barn.

Laughter, as sweet as mountain brook water, washed over him, filled him with relief and peace.

He'd felt a moment's worry when he'd gone in the house after his shift to find it empty. His first thought had been that the baby had come, but then he remembered Lila had said she was going to try to find the toboggan so Brody could try to diffuse some of his son's frantic pre-Christmas energy.

He climbed the ladder quietly, so he could watch them for a moment or two undetected.

Sure enough, they did not see him right away, and he felt his heart expand when he saw Lila laughing at that calico kitten. How was it possible that she could seem more beautiful to him with each passing day? How was it possible that love had no limit, that a man could love more and more and more, endlessly?

Colby spotted him, whooped and tumbled across the loft

toward him. Brody braced himself so that his sturdy son's enthusiastic greeting wouldn't knock him right off the ladder.

"Daddy!" Colby Ethan cried, and leaped into his arms.

Was there any word in the world that made a man feel the way that one did? Ten feet tall and bulletproof?

And soon, another babe would be born. If the doctor was right, on Christmas Day.

Ethan smiled at Lila, and remembered once, it seemed like a long time ago, and a different man completely, he had not liked Christmas.

But now, with his son chattering daily about Santa Claus, and his daughter about to arrive like a special delivery gift just for him, he could barely remember the way it had once been.

Once, a preacher had said the words, *All love leads to loss.*

But now Ethan understood preachers did not know everything, and that one in particular had known less than most.

All love left a mark on the world that made it a better place than it had been before.

This thing inside him as he hugged his son to his chest could never lead to loss. It was the gift that would shape his children, so that someday they would give their gifts to the world. Love didn't lead to loss. Not ever.

"How's the world's bestselling author?" he said, crossing the hayloft with Colby riding in his arm. He sat down in the hay beside her, in no hurry to go anywhere. Home was where she was.

She leaned into him and kissed him right on the mouth.

"Yuck," Colby said.

They both laughed, and then talked about the little things that made up a life: the old farmhouse being freshened up for the arrival of Brody's parents; a postcard from

Jeanie and Karl Jamison that showed Santa's sleigh being pulled by "six white boomers" in Australia; Amanda Murphy, now twenty, and managing Miss L. Toe as if she had been born to it, in the throes of her first love; Mike Stevens flushing the *Be patient, I'm new here* badge down the toilet and flooding the whole police station.

Ordinary moments, ordinary people, ordinary lives.

But everything, especially at this time of year, seeming extraordinary, fused with a light that only a man who had walked in darkness so fully could appreciate.

Brody Taggert looked at his wife's face, felt the warmth of his son nestled in his arms, watched the kittens play and ever so fleetingly felt the whisper of a presence there with them in the hayloft.

Ethan. Love. Something so big and so good it could not be named. But it could be felt, clean through to a man's soul.

He lifted his face to it, closed his eyes and let the pure glory of the moment hold them all.

"You look so happy," Lila whispered, and her fingertips touched his face.

"Well," he said, with a smile, and kissed her fingertips, "You know how I get around Christmastime."

* * * * *

Silhouette Desire kicks off 2009 with
MAN OF THE MONTH, *a yearlong program*
featuring incredible heroes by stellar authors.

When navy SEAL Hunter Cabot returns home for
some much-needed R & R, he discovers he's a
married man. There's just one problem: he's never
met his "bride."

Enjoy this sneak peek at Maureen Child's
AN OFFICER AND A MILLIONAIRE.
Available January 2009 from Silhouette Desire.

One

Hunter Cabot, Navy SEAL, had a healing bullet wound in his side, thirty days' leave and, apparently, a wife he'd never met.

On the drive into his hometown of Springville, California, he stopped for gas at Charlie Evans's service station. That's where the trouble started.

"Hunter! Man, it's good to see you! Margie didn't tell us you were coming home."

"Margie?" Hunter leaned back against the front fender of his black pickup truck and winced as his side gave a small twinge of pain. Silently then, he watched as the man he'd known since high school filled his tank.

Charlie grinned, shook his head and pumped gas. "Guess your wife was lookin' for a little 'alone' time with you, huh?"

"My—" Hunter couldn't even say the word. *Wife?* He didn't have a wife. "Look, Charlie…"

"Don't blame her, of course," his friend said with a wink as he finished up and put the gas cap back on. "You being gone all the time with the SEALs must be hard on the ol' love life."

He'd never had any complaints, Hunter thought, frowning at the man still talking a mile a minute. "What're you—"

"Bet Margie's anxious to see you. She told us all about that R and R trip you two took to Bali." Charlie's dark brown eyebrows lifted and wiggled.

"Charlie…"

"Hey, it's okay, you don't have to say a thing, man."

What the hell could he say? Hunter shook his head, paid for his gas and as he left, told himself Charlie was just losing it. Maybe the guy had been smelling gas fumes too long.

But as it turned out, it wasn't just Charlie. Stopped at a red light on Main Street, Hunter glanced out his window to smile at Mrs. Harker, his second-grade teacher who was now at least a hundred years old. In the middle of the crosswalk, the old lady stopped and shouted, "Hunter Cabot, you've got yourself a wonderful wife. I hope you appreciate her."

Scowling now, he only nodded at the old woman—the only teacher who'd ever scared the crap out of him. What the hell was going on here? Was everyone but him nuts?

His temper beginning to boil, he put up with a few more comments about his "wife" on the drive through town before finally pulling into the wide, circular drive leading to the Cabot mansion. Hunter didn't have a clue what was going on, but he planned to get to the bottom of it. Fast.

He grabbed his duffel bag, stalked into the house and paid no attention to the housekeeper, who ran at him, fluttering both hands. "Mr. Hunter!"

"Sorry, Sophie," he called out over his shoulder as he took the stairs two at a time. "Need a shower, then we'll talk."

He marched down the long, carpeted hallway to the rooms that were always kept ready for him. In his suite, Hunter tossed the duffel down and stopped dead. The shower in his bathroom was running. His *wife?*

Anger and curiosity boiled in his gut, creating a churning mass that had him moving forward without even thinking about it. He opened the bathroom door to a wall of steam and the sound of a woman singing— off-key. Margie, no doubt.

Well, if she was his wife...Hunter walked across the room, yanked the shower door open and stared in at a curvy, naked, temptingly wet woman.

She whirled to face him, slapping her arms across her naked body while she gave a short, terrified scream.

Hunter smiled. "Hi, honey. I'm home."

* * * * *

Be sure to look for
AN OFFICER AND A MILLIONAIRE
by USA TODAY *bestselling author Maureen Child.*
Available January 2009 from Silhouette Desire.

CELEBRATE
60 YEARS
OF PURE READING PLEASURE
WITH **HARLEQUIN**®!

We'll be spotlighting a different series
every month throughout 2009
to celebrate our 60th anniversary.
Look for Silhouette Desire® in January!

MAN of the
MONTH

Collect all 12 books in the Silhouette Desire®
Man of the Month continuity, starting in
January 2009 with *An Officer and a Millionaire*
by *USA TODAY* bestselling author
Maureen Child.

*Look for one new Man of the Month title
every month in 2009!*

www.eHarlequin.com   SDMOMBPA

Silhouette

SPECIAL EDITION™

**The Bravos meet the Jones Gang
as two of Christine Rimmer's famous
Special Edition families come together
in one very special book.**

THE STRANGER
AND TESSA JONES

by

CHRISTINE RIMMER

Snowed in with an amnesiac stranger during a
freak blizzard, Tessa Jones soon finds out her
guest is none other than heartbreaker Ash Bravo.
And that's when things really heat up....

*Available January 2009
wherever you buy books.*

Visit Silhouette Books at www.eHarlequin.com   SSE65427

REQUEST YOUR FREE BOOKS!
2 FREE NOVELS PLUS 2
FREE GIFTS!

HARLEQUIN ROMANCE®

From the Heart, For the Heart

YES! Please send me 2 FREE Harlequin Romance® novels and my 2 FREE gifts (gifts are worth about $10). After receiving them, if I don't wish to receive any more books, I can return the shipping statement marked "cancel". If I don't cancel, I will receive 4 brand-new novels every month and be billed just $3.32 per book in the U.S. or $3.80 per book in Canada, plus 25¢ shipping and handling per book and applicable taxes, if any*. That's a savings of over 15% off the cover price! I understand that accepting the 2 free books and gifts places me under no obligation to buy anything. I can always return a shipment and cancel at any time. Even if I never buy another book, the two free books and gifts are mine to keep forever.

114 HDN ERQW   314 HDN ERQ9

Name	(PLEASE PRINT)
Address	Apt. #
City State/Prov.	Zip/Postal Code

Signature (if under 18, a parent or guardian must sign)

Mail to the **Harlequin Reader Service:**
IN U.S.A.: P.O. Box 1867, Buffalo, NY 14240-1867
IN CANADA: P.O. Box 609, Fort Erie, Ontario L2A 5X3

Not valid to current subscribers of Harlequin Romance books.

Want to try two free books from another line?
Call 1-800-873-8635 or visit www.morefreebooks.com.

* Terms and prices subject to change without notice. N.Y. residents add applicable sales tax. Canadian residents will be charged applicable provincial taxes and GST. Offer not valid in Quebec. This offer is limited to one order per household. All orders subject to approval. Credit or debit balances in a customer's account(s) may be offset by any other outstanding balance owed by or to the customer. Please allow 4 to 6 weeks for delivery. Offer available while quantities last.

Your Privacy: Harlequin Books is committed to protecting your privacy. Our Privacy Policy is available online at www.eHarlequin.com or upon request from the Reader Service. From time to time we make our lists of customers available to reputable third parties who may have a product or service of interest to you. If you would prefer we not share your name and address, please check here. ☐

HR08R

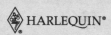

INTRIGUE

Sabrina Hunter works hard as a police detective
and a single mom. She's confronted with her
past when a murder scene draws in both her
and her son's father, Patrick Martinez. But when
a creepy sensation of being watched turns into
deadly threats, she must learn to trust the man
she once loved.

SECRETS IN
FOUR CORNERS

BY

DEBRA WEBB

**Available January 2009
wherever you buy books.**

www.eHarlequin.com

HI69375

Coming Next Month

**Harlequin Romance® rings in the New Year in style this month.
Ball gowns, tiaras and six dashing heroes will ensure
your New Year starts with a bang!**

#4069 LUKE: THE COWBOY HEIR Patricia Thayer
The Texas Brotherhood

In *The Texas Brotherhood* series, Luke returns to Mustang Valley, where blond
beauty Tess is waiting for him—waiting to fight for the place she and her little
daughter call home. The businessman in Luke would evict them without a
care—but the man in him has different ideas.

#4070 NANNY TO THE BILLIONAIRE'S SON Barbara McMahon
In Her Shoes...

It's New Year's Eve. Sam has her hands on the hottest ticket in town, and finds
herself dancing with billionaire Mac! But when the clock chimes twelve, reality
strikes! Her stolen night has cost Sam her job, but Mac comes to the rescue.

#4071 THE SNOW-KISSED BRIDE Linda Goodnight
Heart to Heart

A secluded cabin in the Rocky Mountains is the perfect place for Melody to
hide from the world. But now ex-army ranger John needs her help to find a
missing child—she knows the unforgiving mountains better than anyone. Soon
something about this mysterious beauty captures the rugged ranger's heart....

#4072 CINDERELLA AND THE SHEIKH Natasha Oakley
The Brides of Amrah Kingdom

In the first of the *Brides of Amrah Kingdom* duet, Pollyanna has come to Amrah
to relive her great-grandmother's adventure. Journeying through the desert
with the magnificent Sheikh Rashid feels like a dream! As the fairy-tale trip
draws to an end, Pollyanna's adventure with Rashid has only just begun....

#4073 PROMOTED: SECRETARY TO BRIDE! Jennie Adams
9 to 5

With a new dress and a borrowed pair of shoes on her feet, mousy Molly is
transformed for a posh work party. But will it be enough to catch the eye of her
brooding boss, Jarrod?

#4074 THE RANCHER'S RUNAWAY PRINCESS Donna Alward
Western Weddings

Brooding ranch-owner Brody keeps his heart out of reach. But vivacious
stable-manager Lucy has brought joy to his hardened soul. Lucy has found
the man who makes her feel as though she belongs—only she hasn't told him
she's a princess!

HRCNM1208BPA